BREACH OF PEACE

Book I

DANIEL GREENE

ISBN 9780578840789 (e-book)
ISBN 9780578840772 (Paperback Edition)

Edited by Adam Segaller
Cover art by Felix Ortiz
Book design by Jay S. Kennedy

THE CRIME

The scene at the front door was seared into Khlid's mind: a child, hanging by a chain from the second-story window, his swollen, bloody face confronting her as she approached the manor. Protocol was to leave the location of a crime untainted for as long as possible. Khlid had nonetheless ordered a beat cop to remove the horrid sight—the boy, no older than ten, deserved his dignity—but the chain was thick and the officer was still sawing away.

Now Khlid stood before the servants of the manor, assembled in stunned silence. "We won't rest until the truth comes to light. God bless."

"God bless," the staff echoed, some through tears.

Khlid turned to Rollins, standing behind her,

reached into her coat pocket, and pulled out her notebook. "Have we counted the dead?"

"At least six, ma'am. Still checking all the rooms," Rollins said. The reed-like sergeant was the best the Seventh Precinct had to offer. His age had slowed him down, but he still managed a crime scene better than most. "We are checking the surrounding grounds for anything out of the ordinary. Inspector Chapman is already inside the house making his analysis."

Chapman gets first look. Fucking great.

The next question hurt to ask: "Did we find what was missing of the boy?"

Rollins inhaled slowly before responding. "No, ma'am."

Khlid walked to the house, her head down in thought. Rollins followed close behind. The morning air was wet and cold. The downpour from the night before had evaporated; now all that remained was the mud and fog. Khlid's feet squished along the ground. Considering the manor's distance from the city, Khlid expected to hear morning birdsong, or country hounds barking to protest their disturbed routine. Instead, the land itself seemed to hold its breath, as if haunted by the events from the night before. Against the silent backdrop, the rumble of carriage wheels announced the arrival of more officers to protect the scene.

"How much information do we have on the family?" she asked Rollins, averting her gaze from the front door.

The sergeant pulled out a notepad. "What do you already know, ma'am?"

Khlid thought back to the report she had read in the carriage ride over. "Pruit family. Loyalist to their core. Perfect record on paper. The head of the family, Charl, made his money in manufacturing. Mostly providing for the war effort."

"Providing what?"

"Steel."

Rollins coughed. Khlid realized she was taking a drag from a cigarette she did not remember lighting. The damn things had become as natural as walking. Rollins had made it well known he hated their acrid smell.

"Completely right, ma'am." Rollins turned a page. "One daughter and one—umm..." He glanced at the house. "One son. The matriarch, Muri Pruit, oversaw the import of countless cultural goods to the capital city from across the Empire. Of note, she was recently responsible for acquiring the Royal Stones of Jurridia."

"Fascinating," Khlid said with mock interest.

The southern nation of Jurridia had come under Imperial rule about five years ago. Many of their royal artifacts had been taken to be displayed in the Museum of Kingdoms. "Were they socialites?"

Rollins lifted his gaze from his notes. "Ma'am?"

"How often did they go to those royal parties in the city? You know, the shit rich people live for."

"We don't know that yet, ma'am."

Khlid snatched the notebook from Rollins' hand. She wrote down three addresses, then handed it back. "Find their address book. If any of those are in there, let me know."

"Yes, ma'am."

"And, Rollins."

"Yes?"

Khlid indicated her cigarette. "I'm sorry."

He nodded and headed for a side entrance to the manor. Khlid noticed a workman's shed, roughly fifty meters from the manor. Something that had been bothering her suddenly came into focus.

She walked halfway over to the shed. There was a medium-sized window on each side—but only one reflected the foggy morning light; the other was a dark maw. "It poured rain all last night," she muttered to herself. "What are the chances a family this rich has a staff too sloppy to close a shed window during a storm?"

Khlid tossed her half-smoked cigarette to the ground.

Nasty habit. Really must stop.

She looked around. Every hedge was trimmed to perfection. No forgotten tools lay about. The exterior of the house itself was immaculate. "Unlikely."

Khlid now saw a small padlock dangling from the shed door's latch. "Can't open it from the outside without a key. Can't open it from the inside if it's locked. Which means..." She was close enough now to see that the window had, as she thought, been smashed.

Arriving at the shed, Khlid noted there was no glass on the grass outside. "Smashed inward to climb in. So we have..." She leaned in. "Yup."

Blood on the shed's floor.

"Never climb through broken glass." Khlid pulled out her notebook and noticed another cigarette burning in her hand.

Damn it!

Flicking the cigarette to the grass, she called out, "Bring the cutters." An officer, standing just outside of a small servants' entrance, hands on his knees, looked her way. "Yes, you. Cutters if you would."

The officer jogged toward the front of the manor.

Khlid squatted near the window to inspect a mess of footprints in the mud. They all seemed to be one size—medium, if a male—headed both toward and away from the shed.

What happened was clear. The why remained murky.

Khlid walked around the shed, but found nothing else of interest. A rising sense of impatience grew within her. She was tempted to shoot the padlock off. Logically, it should work, but she had never actually seen it done.

As she began to seriously consider drawing her sidearm, the officer returned with a pair of cutters.

"Thank you, dear."

The officer heaved at the cutters, but only got halfway through the lock. Another heave and the lock gave way with a solid clip. Khlid thought she could have managed it in one. True, she'd had plenty of time and tension to exercise over the last couple of weeks, but she was generally unimpressed with officers' tendency not to keep up with fitness after basic training.

"Well, this is lavish." Khlid had never seen a shed so clean and organized. Granted, she had not been *in* many royal sheds, but this was bordering on ridiculous. She took several beats to take in the room. Clearly, the floor was regularly swept and polished. Most of the tools looked like they had never been used—though this was unlikely, given that the grounds were equally pristine.

Either compulsively replaced or cleaned. More likely cleaned.

"Officer..." Khlid searched his face for a name. "...Smits. What do you think happened at the window?"

The officer looked nervous under her stare. "I assume that's men's footwear in the prints?"

"Yes."

"Only one set?"

"Correct."

"Someone broke in looking for a weapon, I'd say."

"If they were a woman's footprints, you'd have a different theory?" Khlid took another unconscious drag from a cigarette.

"I didn't say that. But—have you met many Imperial ladies, ma'am?"

"I have not had the pleasure."

"They aren't the type to run for a weapon. With the looks of this place, someone would've only come to this shed last night looking for two things: a weapon or a place to avoid death. Only one set of prints, so no chase. The royal men like to think they're heroic. I could see one coming here with a last stand in mind."

"Well done, and I believe you're correct." Khlid wasn't so sure about the officer's remarks on upper-class gender politics, but everything else added up. She came to a stop. "But what tool would I take?" Khlid scanned the whole room once again. With a place this organized, it should have been obvious if something were missing.

"Should I get one of the workers, ma'am? I'm sure a gardener would know the shed well enough to spot—"

"No," Khlid cut in. "We don't want to bring any possible suspects in here until we've swept it repeatedly."

"Right, ma'am. Sorry, ma'am." He paused, humor slipping into his voice. "It looks fairly well swept to me, ma'am."

"Yes, this place is unsettlingly clean." Khlid hardly even finished the sentence. Her mind was focused on the room now, and barely registered the officer.

Even the floor was clean. *Who in the hell cleans their shed floor?* The only signs of disturbance were the broken window and a smear of blood on the sill itself. Likely to have happened as the man climbed back out. Too much blood to be an immediate result of a gash. It had to have welled up over several seconds.

"Okay, Smits, here is what I know so far. A man came down to the shed after noticing something horribly wrong at the house. We know it was not one of the staff; none of them are hiding cuts. This man did not possess a key—probably one of the royal family; they don't carry things like keys to sheds. So, he smashes the window. The door is locked from the outside, so he has to crawl back out the same way he came in, and leaves a blood smear on the windowsill on the way out. I suspect he did this well past midnight, after the rainstorm had peaked. Otherwise all that blood would have washed away.

"What we don't know is what our mystery man snatched. We also don't know if he had been in the house when things went to hell, or if he came home and witnessed it from the outside. Either way, he was trying to be a hero. Shame he's probably dead."

A voice different than Smits' responded, "Well, that was enjoyable."

That voice snapped the world back into focus. A grin spread across Khlid's face. Heart beating just a bit faster, she stood and saw her husband, Samuel.

Samuel had been away three weeks. Sometimes inspectors were called to investigate matters in smaller towns to help maintain justice throughout the Empire. Samuel must have been handed a simple case: one could hardly do more in three weeks than travel to the provinces, turn around, and come back.

Khlid would have run to kiss Sam, but Smits still stood in the corner furiously writing in his notepad. She settled for walking over and giving Sam a hug. He placed his hand on her face before recomposing his professional demeanor, stepping away and looking around the shed.

"I got in this morning," Samuel said. "I went to the station after I saw you weren't home and was told you were out here on a homicide." A grin pulled at his cheeks. It was something Khlid loved dearly about him. He would do whatever it took to be around her more throughout the day, even visit a murder scene, and would do so with a smile on his face.

"You couldn't have been far behind us," Khlid said. "We've barely been here half an hour." After going over her observations, she asked, "Any clue what could have been taken?"

"Soil knife, I would guess," Samuel said. "Nobles are all taught to defend themselves with knives, even if they carry a gun. I don't see a soil knife in here, and if I was going into a house with one or more murderers, I would want something I was familiar with. I believe it was the patriarch, Lord Pruit, himself who came here. Any of the young dead men inside would have already had a knife on them. The older man probably stopped carrying one, even a decorative one, ages ago."

Khlid smiled. Damn, her man was good.

"How many dead inside?" Samuel asked.

Smits looked up from his notes. "The whole family, plus what appear to be two guests. Six in total, but the family was killed... differently."

"How were the guests killed?" Khlid asked.

"Both killed in their sleep with knife wounds to the heart. Two young noblemen. Very efficient kills." Smits paused. "Have you been inside yet, ma'am?"

The image of the boy swinging in the breeze invaded her mind.

Khlid swallowed before saying, "No. I only got as far as the foyer before I had to handle the staff."

"So, you saw the... the daughter?" Smits' face contorted at the memory. The girl, in her late teens, had been splayed across the foyer floor, extra steps taken to brutalize the body after death.

"Yes," she said. "Any word from the medical team?"

"No, ma'am. And the entire family was handled in a similar fashion." Smits' voice cracked. "The killers took their time. Only the guests died peacefully."

Samuel cleared his throat. "Someone with a clear

vendetta, then. First, kill whoever is in your way so you can take your time with the family."

Khlid shook her head. "Disagree."

"What have I missed?"

"More than one killer. The guests in bed. Each killed by a direct stab wound to the heart, but no disturbance? And those are the *least* involved kills. One person could do what was done to the boy, but the daughter? That requires more."

The image of the teenager's splayed rib cage danced in her mind. "Plus—a house full of victims and no escapees."

Samuel cocked an eyebrow. "So, why not a vendetta?"

"I'm fine with the vendetta theory." Khlid raised her hands in mock surrender. "I'm just not so sure it was aimed entirely at the family."

Smits and Samuel exchanged looks. "Does that not look like an extremely personal attack on the family to you?"

"Yes and no."

Smits spoke up. "I'll bite, why?"

"Because you don't leave a display like that for people who are dead."

"Oh..." Samuel's eyes drifted. "This was left for us."

"It must have been," Khlid agreed.

A stillness hung over them, the thrill of the puzzle overtaken by Khlid's revelation.

She touched her husband's arm. "What are you thinking?"

Samuel remained still. He always did when mulling things over. "I think this is a rebel attack. Like what we've seen in the city."

Color drained from Smits' face. "You think it's related to the attack on the market last year?"

Khlid answered, "What happened here was clearly meant to send a message. This will spread. No matter how hard we try and stamp out the rumors, eventually the people will know the royal class has been hit. Hit in an extreme way."

Smits ran a hand through his blond hair, lost in thought.

This was going to be bad. Recently, several attacks had been made against the Empire, all to send *one* message: a powerful resistance still lived. They worked in the shadows, sowing doubt in the sanctity of the Empire. Explosives had been set off in crowded city streets. A shooter had walked into a market within the very capital, and with the help of unknown conspirators, massacred dozens. Last month, four priests of the Ministry of Faith had been lynched on their own land. *This all fits the rebels' bloody pattern.*

"Smits," Khlid said.

"Yes, ma'am?"

"When we get back to the precinct, I need a report on our theories. Mark your missive top priority and confidential, and send it to the Ministry of Defense."

Smits nodded and turned toward the manor, but Samuel grabbed his arm. "No word of this to the other officers. Not until we know more."

Smits hesitated, as if he took offense at the order. "Of course, sir."

Samuel released him.

Khlid drew her husband's attention. "That wasn't necessary. Smits knows to keep quiet."

Samuel grimaced. "I just know how officers can fucking gossip." He gestured towards Smits' receding figure. "The new ones might as well grease their lips every morning."

"Hey." Khlid pulled Samuel's chin towards her. "What's gotten into you today? You love the fresh recruits. I've seen you put your reputation on the line to back even the freshest recruit's theory."

Samuel met her gaze with his black eyes, a rare genetic trait that accompanied equally dark hair that clashed with his pale skin in a stunning way. Wrinkles now creased his face, and his hair showed the slightest thinning at the edges. But Khlid loved that. Those lines were the fulfillment of his promise that they would grow old together. Besides, Khlid now sported a few wrinkles of her own.

Samuel grabbed her hand from his chin and kissed it. He leaned down, and their lips met for several thumps of her heart.

"I'm not sure. Just something in the air today." Samuel backed away and adjusted his coat. "The case in the country was about stolen chickens."

Khlid had to process what he said, then burst out laughing.

"The local sheriff asked for an inspector for a case about stolen chickens?"

Samuel smiled at the absurdity as well. The letter the precinct received from the sheriff had been oddly cryptic. The chief had debated for an entire afternoon whether the case was worth sending an inspector. Clearly, he had made the wrong choice.

Samuel reached into Khlid's coat pocket for a cigarette. "Over thirty birds, gone without a trace." He lit a cigarette.

Khlid lit up her own. "How the fuck do you steal and hide thirty birds?"

Samuel blew out a puff of smoke and said, "I left my second there to figure out just that."

Khlid, in the middle of a drag, coughed it up with

laughter. "You left your apprentice there alone to deal with farmers?"

"He's a bright kid." A mischievous grin sprouted on his face. "I'm sure he can handle it."

ONCE THEY ARRIVED BACK at the manor, any trace of humor had left them both. The steel chain had finally been cut and the boy was being placed on a stretcher. The chain had been locked tightly around a support beam inside. It had taken two officers and ruined several tools. Men from the medical team now worked to get the boy's injuries documented and his cause of death confirmed. Due to the amount of trauma to the body, Khlid doubted it was the hanging that had ended his life.

They watched, only a few meters away, as the examination was conducted on a table brought by the medical team. Several moments passed before Samuel said, "Did you order him down?"

"Yes," Khlid replied.

Samuel was silent.

"I know it—" She inhaled. "It might mess with some evidence. But I can't leave a ch—"

"You made the right call," Samuel cut in. "We can't be animals like them." They stood apart now, but Khlid reached out and squeezed her husband's hand, just once.

A member of the medical team, dressed in an all-white uniform, came from the house with a tray of what looked like body parts. Samuel whistled and caught the man's attention, waving him over.

"The boy's?"

The medical man wore a mask, but his voice alone conveyed rattled nerves. "We believe so."

Samuel reached into his pockets and put on a pair of leather gloves. He began his own examination of the body parts, lifting one from the tray of the medical man in front of him.

The man began to protest, "Sir, do you really—"

"Yes." Samuel did not even look up. "No offense, but once you start with those preserving agents, a lot is lost."

As Sam went over a portion of an arm, a foot, and something Khlid could not recognize, she stepped over to watch the examination of the hanged boy more closely. The two medical men rolled the boy over on their table, revealing several puncture wounds on his back. More notably, the child's head lolled at an unnatural angle.

Khlid's stomach heaved at the sight, forcing her to look away. *I can do this with adults, but Almighty...*

Averting her gaze from the brown-haired child, she decided to simply ask one of the two working what they had found so far.

The woman maneuvering the child's body answered Khlid's questions. Khlid scribbled furiously—some of the medic's insights were actually decent. The cause of death was almost certainly the puncture wounds on the boy's back. They bled the most, and were messier than the rest. His arm had been severed at the elbow. Chunks of flesh, ripped away from the stomach and left calf, while gruesome, were not as bloody as might have been expected.

"And the eye?" Khlid asked.

"That we don't know." The woman's voice remained cool and smooth. "No one's found it yet."

"Thank you." Khlid meant that in multiple ways. Medical teams were dedicated to saving lives. Being called to a scene like this was, she knew, doubly painful for them.

She walked back over to Samuel. "What did you see?"

"You're right. This was for us."

Khlid couldn't help but look back at the boy. "What confirmed it for you?"

"That arm was ripped from its socket, not cut." Samuel removed his gloves and dismissed the man with the tray. The medical man walked over to a chest filled with ice and began carefully placing the pieces inside. "One sick freak might do that for pleasure. But the whole family was done like this, or worse. You're right, Khlid. This was the opposite of a crime of passion. This was a whole night's work for a team of people."

"I saw the same on the trunk of the body. He was probably killed quickly from being stabbed repeatedly in the back." She finally decided to button her coat completely to fight the chill. "I suppose calling that a blessing would be inappropriate."

"Yes, it would." Samuel sighed and then did something they'd both been avoiding: he walked toward the entrance to the manor. Khlid let out a long breath of her own and followed him in.

ONCE INSIDE THE MANOR, Samuel stopped abruptly, stiffening. Khlid assumed the sight of the brutalized girl had gotten to him. If that was the case, she could hardly fault him. Even the most experienced inspectors struggled with harm to kids. But Samuel was not looking at the girl splayed across the floor—he was staring at Inspector Chapman.

Chapman was tall, dark, and what any woman would consider handsome. He pulled off the bald look extremely well, and the uniform seemed to carry extra authority on his shoulders. Unlike most members of the force, he also bore many tattoos. Intricate designs littered his arms and hands, blending into his dark skin. With his coat off and sleeves rolled, the ink was an immediate draw for her eye. Khlid found herself wondering if the ink went past his forearms.

Samuel and Chapman had the same kind of rivalry schoolboys did. It had started all the way back in basic training. It had even come to blows. Twice.

"Does he really get under your skin that easily?"

"Why is he even here?"

"You're lucky it's just him." More annoyance slipped into Khlid's voice than she intended. "As soon as they heard a royal family was murdered, half the inspectors on the force tried to glom on to this case. They wouldn't stop badgering me until the captain actually ordered them to stop."

"So why did *he* get through?"

"You know why."

Samuel only grunted in response and walked over to Chapman.

Chapman glanced up from the body of the girl briefly to say, "I'm busy, Sam."

Khlid could hear the displeasure in Samuel's voice as he said, "Have you found anything?"

"*Busy.*"

"Chapman."

Chapman sighed and stood up. He removed his leather gloves, walked over to a nearby table, and dropped them there. He pulled a roll of cigarettes from his pocket, lit one, and took a long drag before turning back to Samuel. "Yes."

Samuel let out an exasperated sigh, looked back to Khlid leaning on the doorway, and pleaded for help with his eyes.

She smirked and said, "Oh, you cracked this egg; you deal with it."

Chapman tossed her a grin. Khlid did not mind Chapman half as much as her husband seemed to.

Samuel struggled with the fact that while Chapman was arrogant, younger, and clearly sloppier at the job as a whole, he was undeniably a better inspector. Chapman had the highest rate of solved cases in the history of policing. Not just the highest in her precinct, either—the highest on the entire continent.

Samuel squared his shoulders. "Would you care to elaborate?"

"If we must!" Taking in the room, Chapman made a sweeping gesture with one arm that nearly smacked the cigarette out of Samuel's hand. As he did, Khlid noticed a slight tear by Chapman's right jacket pocket. "Where to begin?"

He made a show of looking at the corpse of the girl, to the bannister above, and back to the girl's feet. Chapman then squatted low and stared intently at some blood smears before stepping over the body and walking into a small study.

Khlid followed him in first. Grunting in displeasure as his wife reached Chapman's side, Samuel hastened after them.

By the time Samuel entered the study, Chapman was already sitting in an armchair, posing with a book he'd plucked off the nearby shelf. He sat there pretending to read for several seconds.

Samuel let out a cough.

Chapman looked up from his book feigning surprise. "Yes?"

"You were going to elaborate?" Samuel said. "Or am I meant to infer your thought process from the obnoxious show you just put on?"

An air of competition filled the room. Chapman made a pistol with his fingers and shot an imaginary bullet at Samuel. "Spot on."

Samuel narrowed his eyes. "Well, I saw the girl's neck bent pretty severely."

"Correct," Chapman responded. "But not just her neck."

"You gestured up to the bannister," Khlid cut in. "You think she was thrown off?"

Chapman exhaled, letting the book drop to the floor. "No."

Both Samuel and Khlid paused.

Khlid spoke first. "Chapman, you think this girl jumped on her own?"

Chapman met her eyes for the first time. "I know she did."

"How?" The light of intrigue replaced the competitive edge in Samuel's eyes. He took a chair across from Chapman. "How do you *know* the girl jumped?" He emphasized the word "know" heavily.

To his credit, Chapman seemed to forgo the stage-play for the time being. He replied simply, "Blood smears. The girl dragged herself several paces from where she landed. Why not walk? Her legs were broken. If you're thrown from a bannister, it's extremely unlikely you'll land cleanly enough to break *both* your legs. Much more likely if you jump." Chapman emphasized the word "both" in an imitation of Samuel, who either let it go or was too deep in thought to notice.

"So someone chases her upstairs. In a desperate attempt to get away, she flings herself from the bannister. Lands on her feet, but wrong..."

"She never had a chance to land right." Chapman was leaning back in his chair with fingers steepled. Khlid could tell he was comparing Samuel's mental conclusions to his own.

That was the damned irony: when these two worked together, the results were amazing.

"Ah, yes," Samuel replied. "Ladies' shoes hardly make for secure footing." Samuel leaned back in his own chair as he put together the rest of the scene. "She lands from the fall and snaps one or both of her legs. Unable to get up, she desperately tries to drag herself to the door. Whoever is chasing her catches up, breaks her neck, and begins the mutilation."

Chapman furrowed his brow. "What makes you think the neck was first?"

Samuel leaned forward. The fact he had caught something Chapman missed brought the light of competition back into his eye. "One: it fits a pattern. The two guests, the men found in bed together, were killed quickly. The little boy outside killed with rapid stabs to the back. That alone would lead me to believe the girl was as well, but on top of that, point two: the blood on her is wrong."

Khlid kicked in, "The gore is all localized, Chapman. She wasn't fighting when they tore her apart. The blood smears lead up to a relatively clean site. How did you miss that?"

Chapman let out a grunt and said, "I was just getting there when the smell of your husband interrupted my cogitations. Overwhelming everyone with your cologne is not a substitute for bathing, did you know that, Samuel?"

Samuel gritted his teeth. "I've been on the road."

"Oh, you've been gone?" Chapman stood. "Well, we have a manor to investigate. How about you two take the upstairs and I'll take the cellar. Meet in the middle, about, I don't know..." He rolled back his sleeve, consulting a non-existent watch. "Lunchtime?"

As Chapman had risen, his coat opened just enough for Khlid to notice the holster at his hip, empty. Samuel rolled his eyes and began to walk from the room. Khlid grabbed him by the shoulder, stopping him in his tracks. Samuel looked at her, confused, but Khlid's eyes were fastened to Chapman. She wasn't sure how, but she knew she was about to catch him in a lie.

"Why is your coat torn, Chapman?"

Chapman paused imperceptibly before saying, "Ripped it last night in a chase. Horrible timing, really. The bastard got away and everything."

Khlid held his gaze as she stepped forward. "It must have been a remarkably fast suspect, Chap." She gave him a sickly-sweet grin. "Everyone knows you're the fastest one on the force."

"Hm." Chapman was always ready with a retort, yet he paused. "Guess he must have been."

"Hm," Khlid said, and took her husband forcefully by the arm, all but marching him out of the room.

2

THE MADNESS

The rest of the house was like a museum of gore and death: bits and pieces of the victims had been left on display for Khlid, Samuel, and Chapman to find and examine. If the two children had been left as a signal flag, then the matriarch and patriarch of the family were what they signaled.

The wife was found in the master bedroom, her arms and legs bound to the canopy bed, each limb now bent in a stomach-turning fashion. Naked, skinned, her insides distributed across the room. Her heart lay on the dresser in a pool of blood. Her femur had been roughly torn off and left on the floor. As with the other victims Khlid had seen so far, there was surprisingly little blood. She had been dead before they really got to work on her.

A particular blood stain on the pillow caught Khlid's eye. She leaned in close to peer at the woman's cheek.

Samuel appeared next to her. "They haven't gotten the cellar open yet. It appears to be locked from the inside. The first officer claims he heard movement down there. The lot of them are spooked." Noting his wife's preoccupation, he leaned in close to look at the same markings and stain that had caught her eye.

Samuel's brows shot up. "Well, shit. Is that a bite mark?"

Khlid nodded. "Someone bit this woman's face and spat the flesh out on the pillow."

Samuel took a step back from the bed and rubbed his neck. Khlid turned from the body and gave her husband a once-over. His shoulders were tense, his brow fixed in a furrow.

"You okay?"

"I will be. Have we found any trace of the husband?"

"Well." She pulled out her notes to add a few thoughts. "From what you've just told me, I'm guessing we might find him in the cellar."

"That is what I feared."

"Why is that?"

Samuel grinned. "Chapman is trying to get it open. If there is a panicked man down there..."

"Ah." Khlid closed her notes. "We should get moving."

CHAPMAN HATED when things would not open for him. He tugged on the cellar door, harder this time, but it still refused to budge. "Damn fucking thing." Chapman looked to Rollins. "Do we have anything that goes boom?"

Behind him, Rollins let out a cough. "I don't believe that will be necessary. May I, sir?"

Chapman stepped back, holding his arms wide. Rollins took his place, crouched down, and pulled a lock-picking set from his coat pocket. After a few seconds of trying at the keyhole, he stood up straight and let out a confused "Huh."

"Problem?" Chapman asked.

"It's not locked, sir."

Chapman's eyebrows went towards the ceiling. "So the door is barred. That can only be done from the inside. That confirms the man who claimed there was a noise. *Crowbar!*" Rollins jumped at the sudden volume of his voice. "Do we have one coming?"

An officer by the door called back, "Yes, Inspector."

Rollins' hand unconsciously rested on his service revolver as he said, "Some manors do have secret exits, sir."

Chapman let out an exasperated breath and said, "Rollins, you're good at your job, but there is a reason you're not an inspector."

The other officer bringing the crowbar halted at the statement, and gave Chapman a reproachful look.

Chapman caught the look. Self-admonishment flickered across his face. He turned to Rollins, now frowning deeply at the door. "I'm sorry, Sergeant." Managing sincerity, he added, "I was well out of line. You know I wouldn't say it if it were true. I often say things I do not mean because I think they are funny. That, in hindsight, was not."

"Aye, sir."

Chapman could tell his words were not enough. Rollins had tried for the rank of Inspector many times in his career. Each time, he had fallen just short on several key tests—the ones designed to assess deductive reasoning. Rollins never did all that badly on the tests; just enough to guarantee his superiors would never promote him.

Chapman doubted there was a secret way out of the manor. If there was, whoever had locked themselves down there would have taken it by now, and reported the murders themselves. But seeing the hurt still in Rollins' eyes, Chapman let it go.

The crowbar arrived. The officer holding it stubbornly tightened his grip at Chapman's first grab, his eyes warning that underlings stick together. The message imparted, the officer released the crowbar at Chapman's second tug, and Chapman got to work.

There were often tensions between inspectors and the regular members of the force. Many officers resented the way the Empire lauded inspectors as the holy hands of justice. A few of the more political officers had even denounced the wide leeway inspectors had to convict and sentence suspects without a formal trial. Some had gone so far as to write articles in the Imperial papers denouncing the practice. Chapman knew his stupid remark to Rollins would be brought up at the next union meeting—he had repeatedly been cited as an example of the inspector class' arrogance.

Fuck me and my stupid fucking mouth.

Chapman stepped back to the thick—*oak, maybe* —door that had been giving them so much trouble. He took out some of his tension by levering the crowbar hard enough to crack the wood. "Rollins, a hand?"

The sergeant stepped up and they both opened the door with a surprisingly loud *crack!*

Rollins swung the door open, and the deepest black Chapman had ever seen greeted the three of them. Impenetrable. Something told Chapman that deep darkness would dominate the cellar even if he brought a team of lanternmen with him.

Rollins stepped up and shouted, "Imperial Police. Make yourself known."

Nothing.

Chapman nodded to Rollins and closed the door. "Well, it looks like we will have to make an entry."

"Shall I fetch a lantern and some men, Inspector?" the officer who brought the crowbar asked.

"Yes..." *What was his name?* "...Officer." *Why do I want to call him Officer Shits?* Chapman knew he needed to make a better effort to know the name of every member of his precinct, but there were just too many. *Thirty officers in total?* He had a hard enough time remembering *anyone* who wasn't an inspector. "Bring two lanterns for me and Rollins. You and..." He pointed to another officer whose name eluded him. "...your partner, prepare to follow us in but stand by for now. We don't know what is down there and I don't trust an inexperienced gun behind me. Give me your pipe, would you?" Chapman finished by snapping his fingers and extending his hand.

Officer Shits frowned at his hand and gave him a dirty look.

I really am a fucking idiot. "Please, Officer."

This somehow seemed to make matters worse. Due to rank, Officer Something had to obey, but he slapped the pipe into Chapman's hand and stormed off, grumbling under his breath.

Rollins said, "I know you mean well, Inspector, but you really are terrible with the men."

Chapman exhaled and said, "I know." He checked to make sure his new weapon was loaded. "Gods, I know."

"They do respect you."

Chapman looked at Rollins. "They do?"

"Of course, sir." Rollins seemed to have completely recovered from Chapman's earlier comment. "The force respects any inspector who can solve cases like you do. It's just that they don't *like* you. As a person."

"Few do, my friend. Few do."

Within the minute, Officer Shits returned with two lanterns and his partner. Chapman decided he could not keep referring to him as "Officer Shits"—it was too likely to come out of his head and onto his lips—and just asked his name. Surprising Chapman, this seemed to be the right call: the officer smiled slightly as he mentioned his name. Not that Chapman heard it: he was too preoccupied with the thought that admitting he had forgotten the name was, it turned out, the more sociable thing to do. *Fascinating.*

Whatever good will Chapman had earned from the nameless officer, he promptly squandered it by opening the door to the cellar again and tossing the pipe down the wooden steps to several loud bounces.

"Oi! Why did you do that?"

Chapman continued to stare into the blackness as he answered. "I'd rather they shoot your pipe than me as I walk down the stairs." The officer nodded. At least there was an explanation.

Just as Chapman began to raise his lantern and head into the cellar, he heard two sets of footsteps descending from the floor above. He lowered the lantern with a sigh.

Rollins, confused by Chapman's hesitation, asked, "Nerves, sir?"

"No, Rollins." Chapman watched Khlid and Samuel turn the corner and approach. "Not the way you mean."

KHLID COULD TELL JUST by looking at Chapman that he was far from thrilled they had returned from their task upstairs so soon. He stared unblinking at them as they approached. One of his little ways of letting people know their presence was unwelcome.

"Cheer up, Chapman. We found plenty of gore for you upstairs." Samuel's tone was somewhere between mocking and sincere. "You can moon over the matriarch's corpse just as long as you want."

Chapman's gaze did not falter.

Khlid elbowed her husband. He let out a small grunt, looked at her, and relented.

"At least let us watch your back."

"Rollins has my back," Chapman sniped. The sergeant let a smile come over his lips.

Khlid stepped in. "Sam, Chap, enough. Rollins, would you like us to get *your* back?"

"Absolutely, ma'am." Rollins' tone brooked no dispute.

Khlid gave Rollins a wry look of thanks. When it came to the childish rivalry between Sam and Chap, the only way to get things done was to exhaust them with professionalism.

Chapman huffed, turned, raised his lantern, and

began marching down the stairs, preferring the unknown blackness to his present company. Rollins followed with Samuel and Khlid right behind.

THE LANTERNS PROVIDED A SURPRISINGLY limited view into the darkness. Khlid felt a chill run up her spine. The further down the stairs she walked, the more surely she felt that this cellar was already occupied.

The pools of light traversed an empty expanse, then finally hit an obstruction: rows upon rows of wine racks, as tall as the cellar's high ceiling would allow. The polished bottles glistened against the seeping illumination. No walls visible. The stairs dropping into the middle racks on all sides. No matter where Khlid's eyes went, the darkness seemed to be trying to claw its way closer. Pulling her pistol from its holster, she prepared for the worst.

Chapman reached the bottom of the stairs first, and raised his own pistol. He drew a breath to call out, but Samuel placed a hand on his shoulder.

Sam addressed the unknown darkness calmly, "We are the police. It is safe now. I promise." He lowered his weapon. "We won't hurt you."

Chapman gave Samuel a curt nod of approval. Rollins handed Samuel his lantern.

Chapman and Rollins went into the far-left row of wine racks, while Khlid and Samuel went right.

Moving into the narrow aisles between the racks, a smell that had first tickled Khlid's nose at the cellar door now became overwhelming. She hated the smell of wine, and the cellar reeked of it, combining poisonously with the pungent odor of wood polish. The stench filled her head.

Checking over her shoulder, Khlid could barely see the light from the stairway. An eerie feeling that the cellar went on forever began to manifest in her mind. They would walk until the little doorway to light was no longer visible, and then it would be impossible to return. She found herself fighting an odd sense of vertigo—an instinctive terror that, were she to try to run back to safety, she would only encounter an infinite hallway of wine bottles.

Khlid's ears were starved for sound. Every scuff of Samuel's boots made her heart leap. Her own breath sounded as loud as ocean waves. Khlid knew this was what adrenaline did, but that did not stop her hands from shaking, or the grip on her pistol from slipping. Her heart pounded so loudly, she began to wonder if Samuel could hear it.

As if responding to her thought, Samuel turned and looked to her. He mouthed, "You okay?"

She nodded.

He placed a hand over his own mouth, signaling for her to try and quiet her breath. She did so, trying to slow her own heart as well. She took a deep, slow inhale, and let it out slowly as she closed her eyes—

I'm in an endless expanse of nothing. I am falling through eternity. Samuel will not be there when I—

Khlid's eyes popped open and she had to stifle a small whimper. *Well, that was a huge mistake.* Samuel still stood within arm's reach, the furrow in his brow deepening.

What is wrong with me? Khlid could get in a shootout with a suspect and laugh about it an hour later, but the overwhelming silence and darkness tore at her sanity.

Something sticky caught her boot. Khlid looked down and saw a small puddle of black fluid reflecting off the floor. As she processed what the liquid might be, a new smell tingled in her nose—one that made her nostalgic for the repugnant mixture of wine and wood. Though faint now, the odor reminded her of a corpse left in the sun too long. Of the part of town where undesirables were left to fend for themselves. Of rot and rancidity. If it had been stronger than a hint, she was sure her stomach would have heaved. She raised her hand to try and get Samuel's attention.

"*Stop!*" Rollins' voice split the air.

Khlid let out a small shriek. Samuel, startled, looked back at her. Rollins' cry had come from far ahead and many rows over. Samuel nodded to her. They brought up their weapons and hustled toward the source of the noise.

Khlid rapidly became disoriented as they plunged further into the darkness. The light from the stairwell became hidden by the tall racks. The lantern Samuel held high shook back and forth violently, threatening to extinguish the flickering pinprick of light within. Khlid was sure if that light went out, she would go absolutely mad.

The deeper into the black they went, the more gnawing the smell Khlid had first noticed at the black puddle became.

As Khlid and Samuel reached the furthest row, Chapman's light spilled into view. He was running away from them, deeper into the darkness.

"Chapman!" Samuel called out. "Where is Rollins?"

Surprised, Chapman came to an abrupt halt and spun to face them, gun up. Seeing it was only Khlid and Samuel, he spun away again, returning to his chase, then stopped, deciding it was useless. He turned back to his unwanted partners, whispering in a hiss, "I had it!"

Samuel hissed back, "Point that somewhere else and answer my question."

Chapman kept his pistol at the ready. "Rollins couldn't keep up when I gave chase."

"You left him?!" Samuel advanced angrily on Chapman.

"It's all right." Rollins' voice came from behind Chapman.

Khlid nearly jumped out of her skin. "God!"

Samuel saw Rollins enter their light from the darkness behind, but he did not break his stride towards Chapman. "No, it is not 'all right.' Chapman, you—"

"*Shut up!*" The violence in Chapman's voice silenced them all. "We are not alone. Positions."

The command was simple, and they all knew how to follow it. Khlid aimed her weapon down the dark aisle from which she and Sam had come. Sam and Chapman stood shoulder to shoulder, their pistols pointing down the unexplored aisle ahead. Rollins passed Khlid, gun raised, backtracking. The rows of wine extending off into infinity were unnerving, but they certainly simplified defense.

Though Samuel had obeyed Chapman's order, he wasn't ready to let the issue go. He glanced back to Rollins and said, "Are you okay?"

"Quite."

Of Chapman he inquired, "So? Did you get a look at him?"

Chapman cocked his pistol's revolver. "'Him'? What I saw was not a man."

Khlid almost broke her watch to look at Chapman. The worst thoughts this cellar had conjured sprang forward.

Something caught Khlid's eye: in the wine bottle closest to her eyeline, the faintest ripple on the surface of the dark liquid within. If she had not been staring directly at it, the movement would have gone unnoticed.

Above her head, she heard a tiny creak. A small voice in the recesses of her consciousness was already screaming. She fought a moment to silence it before raising her eyes.

Khlid looked up and saw a nightmare.

Perched in the half meter of space between the top of the wine rack and the ceiling was the type of thing children feared seeing under their beds. A viper-like face extended out from the cranny on a neck far too long for any human. No lips existed to cover dead teeth, protruding from deeply recessed gums. Eyes blacker than anything nature could have produced. Skinless, writhing fingers, a mess of tendons terminating in bony points. The worst part was its skin. At first, Khlid thought the thing was wearing a baggy robe. As her eyes focused, it became clear those folds were flesh.

A line of spit dribbled from those exposed teeth, and as the demon realized it had been spotted, it emitted a guttural hiss. The noise was just enough to snap Khlid from a hypnotic paralysis.

"Above!" Khlid cried as she whipped her revolver up with one hand and fired. The monster did not move at all in response, but black blood spurted onto Khlid from the wound the bullet made in its shoulder. A sound like countless children shrieking filled the air. It was loud enough to make Rollins drop his weapon and clutch his head.

Samuel tried to react to Khlid's warning, but he seized up at the overmastering noise.

The air vibrated with it.

Only Chapman found the strength to plant himself, aim upward, and fire his revolver.

He missed terribly.

The edges of Khlid's vision began to swim. Her gun hand seemed disconnected from her mind. That shriek was becoming all of existence to her. She wasn't sure how, but she managed to get another shot off.

She hit, if poorly.

The creature's gnarled claw exploded upon impact with Khlid's large-caliber round. Instead of recoiling in pain, it only slumped over and fell from its half-hidden perch. But it continued to shriek.

Khlid saw it would land on her, but the all-consuming noise seemed to have frozen her again. It crashed into her, a wet, heavy mass, and sent Khlid to the cold stone floor. The disfigured face filled her field of vision. She waited for long claws to tear her paralyzed body to pieces. She expected to see that mouth of rotted teeth coming for her helpless throat.

Instead, the shriek became a yowl of pain as the creature spasmed. Blood was flung about as the thing waved its ruined hand in the air. Droplets fell into Khlid's mouth. She tasted rot and death.

The yowl, still the second-loudest thing Khlid had heard in her life, carried a touch less of the concentrated, mind-numbing insanity of the shriek. The difference was just enough to free Khlid's body from paralysis. Her training returned to her. In one smooth motion, she punched her gun barrel directly against the monster's head, and pulled the trigger.

A bucket's worth of corrupted blood splashed over her face. The smell consumed her.

Reality disappeared for Khlid.

"What the fuck just happened?" Chapman's voice seemed to come from across an ocean. "What is that thing?"

"Oh, God. Khlid!" Samuel's voice found her in the void.

A weight was pulled off of her chest. Something began to wipe the foul blood from her eyes and mouth.

"Can you hear me? Khlid, answer me!"

She wanted to answer him, but everything felt... incorporeal. Khlid was adrift. She was not sure where she was or how she got there. Her senses were numb. She had barely felt the massive creature being lifted from her, like a dream half forgotten.

Fingers peeled her eyes open. Samuel's wonderful face appeared before her. She smiled deliriously and said, "Hey, hon." Suddenly, the instinct of panic crashed back in on Khlid. Her dazed eyes shot open. She lunged up, knocking Samuel off-balance and onto his ass. A startling amount of blood continued to pour from the creature's head and shoulder. At least it seemed to be the monster's equivalent of blood, although it was viscous, like the pus of an exploded cyst.

I swallowed some.

The thought sent her to her hands and knees to retch. Three times her stomach emptied itself. Samuel was rubbing her back. Once she was sure her stomach was empty, she looked over to the creature once again.

Chapman donned his gloves and crouched over the gray mass of loose flesh. He lifted its head in both of his hands and seemed to marvel at the continuing blood flow. Without warning, he dropped the head, picked up his pistol from where he laid it on the ground, and shot the thing in the chest two more times.

More black blood than Khlid had thought possible sprayed into the air at each shot. Chapman glared at the thing for a moment, then began to rummage in his pockets.

Samuel broke the silence, "Was it still alive?"

Chapman found what he was looking for, an empty vial. "No."

"Then *why keep fucking shooting it?!*" The three inspectors turned to Rollins, sitting against the wine rack, uncharacteristically panicking. Sweat poured from his brow, and the kerchief he had pulled from his pocket shook violently.

Chapman held the vial to the creature's neck, still dribbling the viscous blood. "Because the blood was still flowing, as if the heart was beating."

"Then it *was* alive!" Rollins exclaimed, more frightened boy than veteran cop.

Chapman did not look up. "No. Just pressure, I believe."

Fluid continued to froth out of the creature.

Samuel looked down to Khlid. "Are you okay?"

She nodded in response, got off her knees, and observed what Chapman was doing. "Please," she said in a rattled voice. "With no fucking snark, explain."

Chapman obliged her. "Look at yourself, Khlid. I've seen the spray from a headshot before, but you haven't been sprayed. It looks like someone painted you. This damn thing was filled like a balloon with... whatever this is," he said, shaking the vial, now full to the cork with black ooze, for emphasis. "Whatever was done to this man, the answers will be right here."

"'Man'?" Rollins asked, regaining a measure of composure.

The sound of a small army of officers storming the basement cut off conversation. Samuel stood up and called out their position, and that the situation had been handled. Khlid watched Chapman pocket the vial and raise a finger to his lips.

Twelve officers arrived, weapons drawn. Samuel showed them the body, which caused one rookie to turn on his heel and vomit. Four men were assigned to keep a watch on the beast while the medical team was summoned. They would take the corpse to the Ministry of Health. After a thorough examination, a report would be sent back to the Seventh Precinct with all the information they could glean.

"We have to finish the search down here, then re-sweep upstairs. I have a feeling this thing's teeth will match the marks on the wife." As Khlid spoke, an image of the creature tearing at her own flesh danced in her mind.

Rollins was busy commanding the men in the cellar to secure the scene, but Chapman and Samuel both turned to her.

"You do not need to worry about that," said Samuel, looking her over. "Get back to the precinct and shower." He looked to Chapman. "We can finish here."

Khlid wanted to protest, but he was right. She was covered in a fluid they had been calling blood—Almighty knew if that was even accurate—and her mind continued to swim. A shower and change of clothes would do wonders. Plus, the eventful morning had already generated more notes and evidence than most cases did in their entirety. Samuel and Chapman would finish up here, and by the time they were back, not only would Khlid be clean, but she would have begun the real part of the investigation: Research. Examination. Deduction.

"Fine. Give me your notes so far and I will." Samuel and, after some pushing, Chapman, tore the morning's pages from their books and gave them to Khlid. Only then was she willing to leave the manor.

Samuel walked her all the way to her carriage. He almost moved to kiss her goodbye, but after failing to find a spot unsmeared by black fluid, settled for brushing some matted hair from her face and an "I love you."

"I love you, too." And with that, Khlid left the last crime scene of her career.

3

THE REASON

Back at the precinct, Khlid used one of the locker room showers. She had to dragoon one of the novice officers into operating the hand pump—the usual attendants had more pressing tasks. Her investigator's cloak was being washed by a recruit. While she preferred the fit of the civilian jacket she now wore, pinning her badge to it felt wrong.

After cleaning up, Khlid secured an investigation room with a large evidence table and a sizable chalkboard. This was all standard procedure now, but she still considered every resource of her job a gift from the Almighty. Decades ago, after the Almighty had secured power, it not only handed down countless extraordinary technological advancements, but replaced the military forces patrolling the streets with civilian policemen, more directly answerable to the community they would serve. Initially, many protested the idea of a citizen law enforcement body; but the entire experiment had worked out wonderfully.

Now Khlid was proud to follow any rule and procedure the Almighty cared to lay down. Beginning a case was an almost holy experience to her. She felt herself drawn closer to the Almighty by carrying out its will through the system it had created.

Now, children didn't grow up wishing to be soldiers, but officers. Even low-level patrolmen were treated with respect. Since their founding, The Capital Police had been a force for good in the community. Those who had been among the first to join were all heralded as local heroes. The captain of the Seventh, Khlid's boss, was one of them.

Captain Williams had mentored Khlid, Samuel, and Chapman since their recruitment. Williams was firm, bordering on brutal with new cops, intent on weeding out the weak stomachs. As a result, his legacy was damn near flawless. He'd brought down several major gangs, for which he received the Medal of Valor from a member of the Anointed, and deployed generations of his loyal protégés in performing community outreach, building and staffing soup kitchens and homeless shelters. The captain did not believe an officer's first duty was to go after criminals. Instead, he trained the Seventh to better the community first and above all.

Khlid wasn't sure this approach to policing would ever have occurred to her, but the results spoke for themselves. The Seventh Precinct's jurisdiction had the lowest crime rate in the entire city.

The captain's most recent goal was the drawdown of military presence within the city itself. He argued in the city paper run by the Ministry of Truth that the police provided all of the security needed for capital citizens, and that the bad old days, when legions of troops would unilaterally announce and brutally enforce crackdowns for any minor infraction, clashed with the purpose of the Capitol Police. The Imperial paper had praised the captain as a beacon of demilitarization in the postwar Empire.

Just that past Monday, the captains of two struggling precincts had even come in to get advice from Williams. Khlid was extremely proud to work for her captain—usually. Right now, she wanted to bite his head off.

"So let me get this straight. You have in your official report that a monster fell on you?" Williams sipped tea as he watched her lay out evidence from the manor on the display table. He had offered to help on site, but, thinking of his age and constant limp, Khlid had politely declined. One doesn't become the most respected man on the force without leaving his youth behind him. Williams spent most of his days organizing community efforts or overseeing the inspectors. Khlid wished he would focus on the former now.

"Captain, I know what the fuck fell on me. I can still taste the damn thing's blood—or whatever that was inside it." They had been going at it for a while now. "The medical team took the creature directly to the Ministry of Health."

The captain took a loud slurp of his tea, swallowed, and said, "Demons were killed off entirely from this region over a hundred years ago. Do I need to take you back to school? Enroll you in first-grade history class?" He gestured sarcastically past the pool of desk officers and toward the exit.

"It wasn't a demon." Chapman's voice came from behind Williams.

The captain greeted him with a nod. "Don't tell me you're here to corroborate this. We don't file reports on demons in cellars."

Chapman slid past the captain and nodded to Khlid. "No, Captain. But"—he pulled the vial of fluid from his pocket and tossed it to Williams—"something horrific was done to the lord of the manor. Something that will certainly be in my nightmares."

"That *thing* was Lord Pruit?" Khlid could not believe it.

Williams had a genuine look of shock on his face. This was his third surprise of the morning: first, the horrific murders of an Imperial family. Second, Khlid, one of his most trustworthy inspectors, returning from the scene to describe a suspect out of a fairy tale. And now Chapman, backing up the insane story.

Chapman pointed to the vial he had tossed. "You had to have seen her come in covered in that. What did you think it was?"

The captain held the vial up to the light from the broad window and said, "Mud."

Chapman shook his head and said, "Age is a bitch."

Williams fixed Chapman with a sharp eye. "Because a *young* man would have *no* trouble looking at a vial of dark liquid and determining it was the blood of an Imperial lord who, it turns out, is also a monster. You're right, Chapman, I must be getting slow."

Chapman grinned in response.

"Chapman," Khlid said, "what could have done

that to him? Hell, how do you even know it was Lord Pruit?"

"No clue what did it to him, but it was him. After you look past the stretched-out skin, the..." Unusually, Chapman seemed unwilling to list the former Lord Pruit's other horrifying traits. "...Other oddities, the man was under there. We also found a necklace, the kind only Imperials wear, underneath all those... folds." To the captain, Chapman said, "This one is above our pay grade; it's going to have to go up the chain. The military will want to take charge of anything to do with the rebellion."

"Chapman!" Khlid could not believe what he had said. "The *police* protect the city. *We're* responsible for finding out what happened here and—"

The captain cut her off. "You're both right." He put his now-empty mug down and said, "Every bit of this is going to the Ministry of Defense." He glanced at the vial of black fluid. "And the Ministries of Health and Truth. But inspectors have jurisdiction to investigate anything and everything that happens within their district. You two keep working this case —Samuel, too. You keep me in the loop, and I'll do the same for the Ministries. Almighty help me."

Khlid could not hide her smile. "Yes, Captain." To her surprise, Chapman said it with her.

Williams glanced at his pocket watch. "I have a

meeting with some stooge from the M.O.D. Let me know what other nightmare fodder you turn up."

The captain left the two of them. Chapman turned back to the evidence table.

"What the hell are you thinking?" Khlid asked. "You bullied your way onto this case; now you want to hand it to the military? This is the most interesting thing we've encountered in years. Possibly ever."

"No, it's not." He waved a hand at her. "Don't you remember the rogue Grip? Far more interesting."

"That was six years ago." She couldn't hide her annoyance.

Chapman cocked his head. "Was it really?" Khlid's eyes bore into him. "Look," he offered. "I don't know. I just don't want to handle this one."

"What is going on with you?"

"I can't think what you mean, Khlid." His eyes remained hooded, scanning the table of evidence and notes.

"You never give up cases. You have a petty assault sitting on your desk from over a year ago." Khlid kicked the table to get him to look at her. "Really think you're going to solve that one?"

"Already did. The mugging never really happened. Old man just wanted attention."

"Sure." She started examining the evidence

herself. A written statement, given by the house-keeper who had first found the hanging boy, caught her eye.

Chapman's eyes remained glued to the evidence table of the case he'd just disavowed. After a few minutes, he took a seat and began writing in his notes. *Good*, Khlid thought, her annoyance at finding him horning into the manor now forgotten. After the terror and violence of the morning, she'd take the help—particularly if it kept the military out of her way. Khlid *did* like working with Chapman at times. He cared about the work and could be genuinely funny. He simply had the social ability of a sea eel.

"Where is Samuel?"

Chapman looked up from his notes and into her eyes—something, she realized, he rarely did. "He stayed at the M.O.H. I believe he wanted to watch the full inspection. Read this." Unexpectedly, Chapman produced a folder from his coat and slid it over to Khlid.

Khlid opened the folder and found two sets of documents: the first, the Pruit family's record of service to the Empire; the second, a record of their finances over the past few years. Chapman had to have taken these from the manor, breaching the protocol for evidence collection. At first Khlid only scanned the documents, but after a few key facts became clear, she read in earnest. The last few lines of the financial report drove her to actually stand and begin pacing the room.

Lord and Lady Pruit owned and operated well over two dozen steel manufacturing plants. After they married, the two had united their dual fortunes to open plant after plant for over a decade. The war effort assured a ravenous demand for steel, which the Pruits provided exclusively to the Empire, assuring their martial superiority and enriching the already-wealthy Pruits beyond compare.

The financial report in front of her showed an extremely dependable relationship between the family and the government; that is, until about two months prior.

Two months prior, one of the family's plants had increased its steel production by over *six thousand percent*. Not only had this one plant produced enough steel in two months to launch an armada; the family itself had made more money in those two months than in the entire two years before them.

"They were about to become the wealthiest family in the city."

"No," Chapman said. "In the *Empire*."

Khlid collapsed into a chair. "The rebellion just slaughtered the Empire's most valuable family."

"Not exactly." Chapman's voice was slow and

extremely calm—a tone he took on when thinking very carefully. "The plants are safe as far as we know. The Empire would have massively increased security before this."

"'This' *what*?"

"Steel manufacturing is chemistry. An increase like that only comes with a scientific breakthrough." Chapman leaned forward. "I have no idea how, but this family is responsible for one of the greatest scientific—"

Khlid finally saw an opportunity to cut off Chapman and correct him, and by God, she took it. "No!" she said, perhaps a little too enthusiastically. Chapman stared at her with open surprise. "Who says the *family* made the discovery?" she continued. "They are clearly trusted by the highest levels of government. Let's say someone at the Ministry of Science makes this breakthrough. They see the military applications. Who do they bring it to?"

"Ah..." Chapman put a finger to his lips. "Right you are. Far more likely."

Khlid pushed on, "Word gets out. The secret is loose. Now, just a couple of plants can supply all of the military's steel. Hell, if this method were common knowledge, steel would never be wanted for again—its price would drop to a fraction of what it was. We could pave the streets with it."

Khlid looked at the evidence on the table in a new light. The message had not been left for the police. The rebellion did not care about them. It had been stupid to think so in the first place. It was a message for the military, and the message was painted in the blood of a royal family: *We know. And we have a weapon of our own.*

Maybe this should *be handed to the M.O.D.,* Khlid thought.

"Something here is still missing but I can't pin it down." Chapman abruptly stood up and walked to the door. His disavowal of the case was clearly forgotten. Every inspector had that weakness. Provide them a mystery and the obsession would take over.

"Where are you going?" Khlid said.

"I have contacts who might be able to tell me something about that blood. Wait for Samuel, then meet me in the West Market by that fat fruit vendor in two hours." He gave her an overblown wink. "I think we've been underestimated. I think we are going to crack this one right open."

"Take Smits with you."

"Who?" Chapman had come to a full stop and was again staring at her. She could never predict what would catch his attention.

"Officer Smits. He was at the manor this morning. I believe he got back just before you."

"Ah! *Smits*. Not Shits."

"Excuse me?"

Chapman ignored her question and opened the door.

Khlid almost went after him. The insufferable egomaniac was going to investigate the most dangerous enemy of the Empire without a partner or even an officer escort. God, she loathed him sometimes. But she did need to hear what Samuel had to report. So she sat back down and took a deep breath, turning from the irritant back to the evidence.

The trouble with solving a crime was there was never just one puzzle; not even in the most straightforward of cases. Just as different witnesses gave differing testimony of the same events, different players on her side had their own takes on how the puzzles should best be solved; it then fell to Khlid to reconcile all the perspectives and piece together the objective picture. Most of the time, she was confident she'd gotten it right. No matter how horrible the crime, solving it let her rest at night. But when working those cases in which self-doubt had wormed its way into her consciousness, she would stare at the bedroom ceiling for hours every night. The more horrific the crime, the less rest.

Maybe an unleashed Chapman is exactly *what this puzzle needs.*

She pulled a cigarette from the pack in her pocket, lit it, took a long drag, and prepared for the hardest part of her job. Piecing all of this shit together.

Within the hour, Samuel had walked into the investigation room, plopped down in a chair, and let out an exaggerated groan.

Khlid grabbed his chin and gave him a kiss. He looked at her and smiled in response.

"Way more appealing without the..." He made a circle around his face with one finger.

She shuddered and said, "Let's not mention that ever again. What did they find out at the Ministry?"

"Fuck if I know."

She looked up at him. "Explain."

Samuel rubbed his forehead with one hand and unbuttoned his long inspector's coat with the other. "As soon as we brought that thing in, their specialists came out and barred us from following." He picked up one of the folders on the evidence table. "I just spent the last hour and a half arguing with a team of armed guards, all suddenly struck mute."

"Members of the Red Hand?"

Samuel shook his head. "No. Those new fuckers. The ones called the Fist. The *elite* of the elite."

Khlid stared at him for a moment. "You just got into an argument with the Fist?"

"More like performed a soliloquy for them."

Khlid decided to ignore the stupidity of her husband's actions. The Fist were literally above the law. If they'd shot him, even unprovoked, it would have been legal. "So they won't tell us anything?" She started rubbing her head.

"No. And I wouldn't expect to hold on to this for long," he said, gesturing to the evidence on the table. "What is the point of having an inspectorial force? Whenever something truly interesting happens, the military takes over and hides it."

"Well, I wouldn't get too discouraged just yet." She explained how the captain had given them permission to investigate anything within the precinct borders, and the new details she and Chapman had ferreted out.

After it was all laid out, Samuel leaned back in his chair and looked at the roof. "Well."

"Yeah, this is big."

"Agreed. Bigger than us. They were right to take it." Samuel got up and looked out the window.

"Excuse me? Chapman hesitates and now you?" Khlid could not believe what she was hearing.

Samuel leaned against the sill and held his hands up defensively. "Don't get me wrong. I want to get to the bottom of this, but now that I see the whole case, it really *is* a military matter. They'd be right to take it. If this involved rebels, it's a threat to the whole Empire, not just our jurisdiction."

Khlid had to pick her jaw up from the floor. How could he say that? Samuel was always pursuing the "wrong" cases. The captain himself had been forced to pull him off of several for one political reason or another. Khlid was the one constantly reminding Sam of the rules. One military stonewalling and he was ready to back down? Capturing all of those thoughts concisely, Khlid remarked, "That is a fat load of shit."

Samuel stifled a bit of mirth. "Excuse me?"

"Since when have you backed down from a case? You follow leads beyond our jurisdiction all the time; even into other cities!" Khlid tried and failed to hide the anger in her voice, though she did manage to stop her foot from tapping—too much.

Sam looked up and exhaled. "This just feels

dangerous. You already had..." He struggled to find the words. "Something attacked you."

A piece of the puzzle slid into place in Khlid's mind. "Sam."

His shoulders hunched. "This was different."

"It's not, though." Understanding replaced her frustration. "I have been shot at loads of times. A bullet would kill me just as much as a... claw."

"You were covered in blood."

She exhaled, knowing the next step in this dance, and said, "I'm fine."

Sam shot back, "But you might not have been!" He seemed to be struggling to maintain his breath. A look of deep unease took hold in his eyes. "Khlid, there was so much blood."

They had had this fight before, from both angles. She had been irrationally mad at him for almost dying, and Sam had returned the sentiment on more than one occasion. This tension came with mixing marriage and work. This work, anyway.

Khlid wrapped her arms around her husband. He reciprocated, and after a moment, she stepped back. Sticking her arms out to the sides, she turned, letting him look at every angle of her. "See? All okay."

He responded with a soft chuckle.

"We don't need to go over this again. Your nerves

are on edge. By tomorrow, you'll be over it and remember that I am fucking bulletproof."

"Oh, *please*."

"Hey, between the two of us, who has actually been shot?" Even mentioning it as a jibe, Khlid flinched at the memory of Samuel taking a bullet to his gut.

"That was only because I was the first one through the door. If I was the *senior* inspector like yourself, it never woulda happened."

"Solve more cases and maybe one day you will be. I might even write you a recommendation."

"The captain is just fond of you."

"He has impeccable taste." Khlid looked at a clock on the wall. "We need to meet Chapman."

"You said he wanted us there in two hours? We'll be early."

Khlid picked up her civilian coat and tugged it on. "Yeah. I want to catch him in the act."

Samuel raised his eyebrows at her. "In *what* act?"

"Speaking with an informant."

"Informant? Who would Chapman know that knows something about *this*?"

Husband and wife had the same realization as his question hung in the air. "Khlid—does Chapman have an informant with the rebellion?"

"I guess we'll find out soon. But I do have a

feeling Chapman is even further out of line than usual."

THEY MADE it to the market about half an hour before Chapman expected them. If Chapman was conducting some private business here, Khlid intended to violate that privacy, and find out how exactly he had ripped his pocket.

Why is a torn pocket bothering me?

She looked to Samuel at her side. "Go left."

He nodded. "Mm-hm."

The outdoor market had over a hundred vendors, selling everything from sweets to southern-decorated daggers. A tobacco vendor near Khlid eyed her with a toothless, dark-gummed grin, and the black of his mouth suddenly brought back the taste of that putrid liquid from the demon. She heaved, and began to turn away.

"Ain't true what the Health Ministry's saying! Smoking is good for ye. I should know!" The vendor flashed his rotting mouth again.

In response, Khlid pulled open the lapel of her jacket and flashed her badge. The vendor's words were not explicitly illegal—civilians could disagree with the Ministries—but men had been beaten for less.

"I didn't mean..." He stepped further behind his booth. "It was a joke!"

Khlid just raised her eyebrow and walked on. The toothless man would be looking over his shoulder for a week, worried about catching a beating from off-duty cops for seditious thoughts. (Some precincts did partake in such practices. Not the Seventh. They never beat civilians unnecessarily. Captain's orders; orders she agreed with. Mostly.)

Over the next twenty minutes, Khlid scoured for Chapman. He was not at the market—which meant he had sent them here not to meet them, but to know where they would be while he did... something he didn't want them in on. *What the fuck are you up to, Chapman?*

Looking at the large display clock in the center of the market, Khlid knew Chapman had out-schemed her. Ten minutes from now, Chapman would be finished with whatever he had been doing and waiting innocently for their rendezvous. Khlid made her way over to the fat fruit vendor. Samuel already sat on a barrel nearby, munching away on a plump red apple. He seemed content.

"It doesn't bother you?"

Samuel wiped juice from his lips. "Chapman? He bothers me every time he opens his mouth."

"I mean—" She looked down at him as he took another large bite. "Never mind."

"Come on. I can't eat?"

No detective's coat stood out to Khlid in the mass of bodies around them. "You sure can."

Samuel went back to devouring what remained of his apple.

As the market clock hit the appointed minute—a quarter past two—Chapman appeared out of the crowd.

"How is the investigative duo?" Chapman's tone bubbled with forced cheer.

Khlid ignored his question. "What news do you have for us?"

"The murders and mutilations weren't done by the rebels," Chapman said, as though stating an obvious and settled fact.

"Bullshit," Samuel said tossing his defeated apple core to the ground. "It's the only option."

"No, *that's* bullshit."

Samuel stood up, impatience in his eyes. and approached Chapman. "Oh, I can't wait to be talked down to even *more* today."

Chapman stepped close enough to whisper. "Samuel, what imbecile would discuss this *here?*"

Samuel pushed his cheek with his tongue and looked to Khlid as if asking permission.

She shook her head no.

"Good boy, Sammy. Do as Mummy says. Now, there is a pub I like—"

"Chapman!" She was loud enough to make more than a few nearby shoppers turn their heads in alarm. "You will show your fellow officer his due respect," she finished at a lower volume.

Chapman's brain again seemed to catch up to his mouth. He at least had the wherewithal to look mildly ashamed. "Sorry."

Samuel looked Chapman up and down, then lashed out and grabbed his lapel. Khlid thought Sam was finally about to deck his fellow inspector, before Samuel's free hand reached into Chapman's coat and grasped his service revolver. Sam then shoved Chapman back hard, cleanly separating him from the gun. Sam sniffed the barrel. "Recently fired. Definitely within the hour I'd say." He looked to Khlid. "That would require an official report." His eyes went forward again. "So, Chap, where the hell have you been?"

The two inspectors, on the cusp of a public row, were beginning to draw eyes. Too late to switch back to a whisper.

Chapman tried to snatch back his pistol, but Samuel shoved him hard in the chest. Chapman stumbled awkwardly into Khlid, who had to steady them both.

"No, Chap," Samuel said with venom. Khlid eyed her husband for cues of what to expect next— his face bore the same look it had when the two had last come to blows. "Explain how you know what happened at the manor wasn't rebels—and what really happened to your damn coat."

Khlid had no problem whatsoever with Chap taking a few well-deserved shoves from Sam—but the situation was in danger of escalating out of control. She knew Sam well enough to see he was not going to resolve this peacefully. *Sam, your damn temper is why you're not a senior fucking inspector.*

"Inspector Whitkins!" Khlid's use of his formal name shook Sam, briefly, from his mounting rage. She hadn't called him that (not outside of their bedroom, anyway) in years. "Mishandling of a firearm in public. Discussion of classified matters. Disrespect of an officer of the law. Creating a disturbance." She looked to Chapman, rubbing a sore chest. "Assault. Do I need to continue?" Suspects' rights dictated that an officer of any rank must list the crimes witnessed before an arrest was made. Khlid had no intention of arresting her husband—hopefully he knew that—but the message was clear. *Snap out of it, you childish embarrassment.*

Samuel looked at her askance, then at the gun in his hand. The realization that a dozen shoppers had stopped to gawk suddenly seemed to hit him.

Khlid wasn't done. She got in Sam's face, but didn't drop her volume. "You will apologize to Inspector Chapman and return to the precinct at once. Report to the captain exactly what happened here. Am I clear?"

Sam had the audacity to look hurt. *Are you kidding me?* It was he who had created an impossible situation for her; if any superior officer *other* than his own wife had observed this display, Sam would already be in shackles, and his badge in danger. Especially for pulling the gun.

A tense silence. Sam didn't move. Khlid traded volume for venom as she hissed at him, "Was I not clear?"

Well, our apartment won't be pleasant tonight.

Sam turned to Chapman, muttered, "I am sorry," and left without looking at Khlid again. Her husband became enveloped in a crowd that rapidly resumed the day's shopping.

Full of regret and furious with herself for feeling it, she watched him go. The discipline had been more lenient than he deserved, and yet, humiliating one's spouse in public was not something that felt good, no matter the circumstances.

Chapman looked at Khlid, confused, and said, "You did not have to do that."

"Yes, I did."

"Yeah, you did." Chapman turned on the few still staring. "Get on! The show is over!"

SEEKING RELATIVE PRIVACY, Chapman and Khlid made their way to a pub just outside the market and grabbed a booth in the back corner. Patrons were typically required to order drinks to stay, but as they were on duty, and would guarantee no fighting in the establishment while they were there, the owner just smiled and nodded as they helped themselves to a table.

"I am sorry that—"

"Stop." Khlid cut him off. "Yes, you were a dick. You always are. But Samuel was way out of line."

Chapman looked down at a stain on the table. "I don't always *want* to be."

"I know."

Khlid let silence hang in the air for a moment. Then: "You do owe us answers."

Mugs of water were brought, and Chapman drank deeply from his before responding. "I do."

He waited, apparently hoping against hope Khlid would somehow forget the topic and move on. After several minutes of silence, he drew breath.

"An informant."

"No shit." Khlid leaned forward. "But if you had a rebel informant and didn't at least bring that up to the captain, you'd be on the borderline of treason."

Chapman flicked his eyes to hers, then looked away. "Yeah, I would be."

"Fuck you."

"C'mon, Khlid."

"No. Fuck you." Khlid leaned further forward until her stomach pressed against the table. "Sam was way out of line, but only because we expect better of him. *You* go around treating everyone else on the force like shit, every day."

"I don't—"

"Yes, you do." She struggled to keep her voice low. "Even the captain bites his tongue with you because you can dish it but you sure as hell can't take it. Sure, you solve cases. You're valuable. Maybe even extremely so. But you're a morale pit. No one wants to work with you. You and your pathetic lone-badass-with-a-badge routine." Khlid realized she was letting years of irritation with Chapman spill out. "Maybe, if you actually decided to *share* what's in that brilliant brain of yours, some of the officers might not dread being in the same room as you." She sat back, regretting only about half of what she'd said.

After several long moments fiddling with his mug, Chapman replied, "Ouch."

"Yeah. Ouch."

Chapman finally looked up with the most emotion she had ever seen on his face. "It is very complicated."

"What?"

"Being me."

Khlid had often wondered if Chapman were one of those people who simply didn't seem to *have* emotions. At that moment, she realized she had been wrong. He was "off," but at least it appeared he wasn't quite a sociopath. She decided to drop it.

"How did you find this informant?"

"Easily."

She sighed. "Why was it so easy, Chapman?"

"Because the informant is me."

His answer came so quickly, it was a moment before she fully processed it. Chapman had just admitted to being in contact with the shadow organization that had slaughtered hundreds of civilians over the last year, during which time the Empire had failed to capture even one of them. Was Chapman outing himself as a traitor? Khlid could think of no above-board reason he would have kept this secret from the precinct.

As the truth crashed home, her hand darted for her weapon.

Chapman put up a hand. "Wait."

She paused, hand on her holstered pistol. Chapman put his hand down, meeting the other resting atop the table. He knew to keep them exactly where they were; that Khlid would have shot without hesitation at the slightest twitch.

Khlid slipped her finger next to the trigger. "What in the fuck have you gotten yourself into, Chapman?"

"I have a question for you. Put your hand back on the table."

Khlid kept her hand where it was. "After what you just said, I—"

"Answer it, and I will gladly go straight to the captain, tell him everything I know and accept whatever comes. I swear it on the Almighty."

Khlid couldn't unclench her teeth. *This was already the longest day of my life three hours ago.* "What does the Almighty mean to a traitor like you?"

He stared back at her, hurt at the term. *How dare he.*

Khlid's hand began to sweat as her grip tightened on her weapon.

"Are you sure our whole precinct is clean?" asked Chapman.

"Besides *you*, you mean?" she hissed.

"I have been working with *them* for months, and even I don't know for sure who in the precinct might have rebel sympathies."

"Who *else*," she corrected him once more. That hurt look again.

Khlid was struggling to maintain objectivity. "You need to tell me everything *now*."

Chapman scoffed, almost earning himself a bullet in the stomach from Khlid. "Do you really think we have the time for stories?"

Frustration bled into her voice. "Chapman."

He relented slightly. "The rebels did not murder the Pruits."

"Who did?" Khlid asked. Her tense jaw began to ache.

"Okay, listen. Bodies have floated ashore, Khlid. Ones with similar deformities. After blackmailing the right people, the rebels learned of a ship. It's a military cargo ship. It harbors at Dock Thirteen, takes a load from Warehouse Two, and sets sail at night. It returns before morning but nothing is ever unloaded."

"So? Lots of waste is dropped into the ocean."

"Discreetly at night with an entirely M.O.D. crew?"

It was infuriating the way he let a story drip out.

He fixed her with a dry look. "Corpses, Khlid. Desecrated corpses, filled with viscous black blood. Test subjects like Lord Pruit—ones who didn't survive the process. Best the rebels can tell, it's mostly homeless people."

Khlid let the pieces fall into place. "That's impossible. The Empire wouldn't put whatever that shit was into its own citizens. And for what?"

"I don't know why. Because they are taking extraordinary steps to make sure we don't know why." Chapman's shoulders sagged. "Khlid, please think this through. They just used gallons of whatever this shit is on Pruit. We have to go to the warehouse district *now*. A member of..." Chapman waited for a drunken man to go by. "My friends are confident a shipment is going out tonight."

"Friends"? These are lies. Chapman is manipulating me for some rebel plot.

Khlid had heard enough. She stood. "Chapman, get up and keep your hands where I can see them."

More than a few patrons of the pub were looking their way with concern. A bouncer near the front looked unsure how to proceed.

"Khlid, don't do this." Chapman remained seated.

Khlid pulled her pistol out and pointed it directly at him. "Chapman, get up, now." She was being loud deliberately now, loud enough for several nearby tables to hear.

An audible gasp rolled through the pub as patrons noticed the drawn weapon. A few sat confused. Some men stood up and drew knives. Khlid could almost hear the collective thought: *Is that inspector* arresting *her partner?* It would be a scandal for the entire Empire. With a scene this public, Chapman was done. He had no options left but to give in. *He has to come peacefully, right?*

Before she could begin reciting his crimes for arrest, a thought occurred to her. "You got rid of Samuel on purpose. You son of a bitch, you knew exactly what to say," Khlid hissed under her breath. At last, Chapman vacated the booth. She took a step back to stay well out of his reach.

She could tell his mind was racing. Chapman kept his hands up, but his eyes darted about the room. They came to a sudden stop, looking her directly in the eyes. "He didn't exactly make it difficult."

It took actual effort for Khlid not to shoot him right there. It wasn't only the rage she felt at his betrayal; Chapman was deadly. He was easily twice her size, and was one of the few officers who actually worked out more than her. In a pinch, police could usually count on help from armed bystanders—but she had no idea how the bar patrons hovering with their knives would interpret a brawl between two uniformed—*Oh, shit*. All at once, Khlid realized she was in a civilian jacket. She had to keep cool and get Chapman back to the precinct.

His eyes refused to leave hers. Their gray calm clashed with her own brown-eyed fury. *Fuck you, Chapman, for being so calm.*

He was standing now, looking down on her. His raised arms seemed more a threat than a sign of compliance. While Chapman was doing exactly as a citizen under arrest should, the aura about him warned Khlid of a move yet to come. She knew Chapman too well to believe his posture was submissive.

"Khlid." His voice shocked her after a few seconds of silence. "Take me somewhere I can explain." He was firm and calm. Khlid had heard him use that tone countless times in interrogations.

Khlid looked to one of the three men with knives drawn. If they misinterpreted the scene, she'd be done for. "My name is Insp—"

That was all the opening Chapman needed. He

lunged and struck her gun hand down to her side. His right fist smashed into her gut, knocking the wind from her. It was the hardest blow Khlid had ever felt.

She began to drop, but Chapman seized her by the throat, spinning her around and pinning her back against his chest. The cold metal of his pistol pressed into her jaw.

Khlid could feel his tattooed hand shaking as it held her aloft by her neck.

"This woman is a fugitive of the law and has been trying to escape Imperial justice for weeks. She promised me she would come peacefully. Obviously that was a lie. Don't worry, all is under control."

One patron actually let out a single clap before looking around and lowering his hands.

Fuck today to tomorrow and back, Khlid thought, still trying to get air into her lungs. Why had she put on a civilian coat? Why hadn't she changed into a fresh uniform? Glancing down, she saw Chapman had swiped her badge as well, likely before they even entered the pub.

To add insult to injury, the son of a bitch hadn't even tried to disarm her—just pinned her in such a way that she had no hope of raising her gun arm. That *might be good,* Khlid thought. If Chapman had planned on killing her on the spot, he certainly would have disarmed her fully.

Hope so. Khlid twisted her wrist and jabbed the barrel of her weapon into Chapman's kneecap. He grunted in pain.

With what little air she had, Khlid said, "Do you want to be a cripple, Chapman?"

He'll back down.

"No." In a flash, Chapman lifted her, twisted his whole body, and slammed her head against the table of the booth she had just vacated.

Blackness.

KHLID HEARD CHAPMAN'S VOICE. He seemed to be arguing with someone, saying he didn't need help taking his suspect back to the precinct. Semiconscious, she thought illogically, *Why would Chapman need help when I'm here?* Memories came back to her. *Oh.* A maddening headache crested, and pain became her reality for several seconds.

She heard Chapman speak more clearly now: "She's coming to. I really must get going. Thank you again for your assistance, but I order you to go back inside and finish your drink."

Some ambiguous, grumbling chat. Chapman putting his foot down. Footsteps growing distant.

Khlid became more aware of her position. No more than thirty seconds could have passed. She could still hear the bustle of the market. Judging from the pressure in her stomach and pain in her wrists, Chapman had tied Khlid up and flung her over his shoulder. Not exactly a traditional arrest, but who would interfere with an inspector appearing to subdue a dangerous criminal?

Trying to lift her head was a mistake. Pain consumed her again.

She realized Chapman was speaking to her as he walked. She tried to listen through the pain.

"—and now you might not even recover in time to make decent backup. I swear, if I have to retrieve that insufferable husband of yours, I'll—"

Khlid couldn't make sense of the sounds anymore. She had regained consciousness quickly. But *fuck* if this wasn't the first long minute of a headache that would last a week.

There was no point trying to fight Chapman now. She was tied, injured, and disarmed. Even if she could subdue him, without any way to prove her authority, she'd be mobbed by outraged civilians. Wherever Chapman was taking her, she was along for the ride.

It turned out to be a place Khlid had never been: his home.

Chapman took her from his shoulder and propped her up beside him—still carrying her weight, but looking more innocent to his neighbors—and walked her around back.

He wrestled with his keys, but managed to get her inside without having to put her down.

In pain, Khlid failed to retain much about the small house. From the street, she had noted it was half of a duplex, but aside from that, things were remarkably blurry. *How have I worked with you for all these years and don't even know what your cabinets look like?*

"You live close to the market," she managed to get out.

"Indeed." Chapman was placing her on a cold, smooth surface.

Oh, a bathroom. "Chapman, why am I in a tub?"

He was rummaging in the cabinet over the sink. "Because I just gave you a concussion. You might vomit."

"I already knocked that off my to-do list today."

"Allow me to err on the side of caution."

"Fair enough."

He turned to her and pushed a vial filled with purple fluid to her lips.

Khlid looked at it and almost laughed. "If you're going to kill me, Chap, just use the gun."

Chapman appeared briefly guilty. "Killing you is not on my to-do list. I just couldn't let you arrest me. Not tonight. Now, do I need to grab a syringe?"

She opened her mouth and swallowed in one gulp. "Fucking hell, that is rancid."

"Not the worst substance you've swallowed today."

He's got me there.

"Chapman."

"Yes?" He pulled a knife from his boot and cut the cord around her wrists.

"What now?"

He sat on a toilet across from her and just breathed for a moment. "I'm going to Warehouse Two. I will keep my head down and gather evidence on exactly what is happening. With that tonic you just drank, you will be able to walk in under an hour. Go back to the precinct. Tell the captain whatever you feel appropriate. Tell him, if you like, that I am part of a rebel ploy and must be stopped. Or you can tell him the M.O.D. is covering up what they did to Lord Pruit. I don't care. Say whatever you have to; but get every available body out of that precinct and down to the docks. I will need the backup."

Khlid could only stare. It didn't matter that Chapman was manipulating her; she had no choice but to do as he suggested. "You're the largest pain in the ass I—"

"Am I a friend?" Chapman again met her eyes. She returned his stare with equal intensity.

"Yes."

"Then, please, get every officer you can." He stood and dropped her pistol in the empty sink, well out of her reach. "I need help tonight."

And then Khlid was alone. She heard the front door to the house open and close. All she could do was wait for the pain to subside.

Minutes ticked by at an agonizing pace. The only measure that seemed to help was forcing her eyes shut and not paying attention to anything. She floated in an odd meditation for an uncertain amount of time. Khlid attempted to marshal her thoughts on what had just happened.

Chapman had manipulated her and her husband. He had spent months feeding valuable intelligence to enemies of the state. He had just assaulted her. Now, he was walking into a trap—one that, depending on Khlid's actions, would ensnare either Chapman alone, or the entire Seventh Precinct.

Finally, her eyes snapped open. Whatever Chap had given her seemed to have taken hold; the stabbing pain in her head subdued to a manageably dull thump. She was still concussed, but now she could function. Her balance was off and her vision swam, but she could ignore it enough to stand and walk.

She got out of the tub and retrieved her pistol. Making her way to the central room, Khlid saw why Chapman had never brought anyone from the precinct here: it was not a home. It was just where he slept. She could count the number of nonessential items on one hand. No art decorated the walls. One chair. A table large enough for one man to eat at, next to a mattress on the floor. Khlid pulled a cigarette from her pocket and took a moment to pity the man with so little to lose.

A boom of distant thunder cemented the dread in her stomach.

THE MISTAKE

Khlid staggered through the Seventh Precinct's front door, brushed off as much of the rain as she could manage, and was greeted by Rollins, on his way out. Surprised to see her, he said, "Ah. I guess I don't have to go hunting for you, then." He looked at her properly now. "Inspector Khlid, are you feeling alright?"

"No." She tossed her smoke out the door behind her. "Where is Samuel?"

"His desk. The captain reamed him out for a solid twenty minutes. Sam just sent me to make sure you and Chapman had not, as he put it, 'come to blows thanks to how donkey-headed I had been.'"

Khlid left the sergeant and went to find her husband.

Samuel was sitting at his desk, head down and

shoulders slumped. Khlid had seen him in a similar mood countless times before—most often when he was about to give up on a case and hand it to Chapman.

He looked up at the sound of her steps, then stood in dismay at her appearance. "What happened to you? Are you okay?" A darker look came into his eyes. "Where is Chapman?"

"We need to speak with the captain right now."

Without question, Sam walked her to the captain's office on the second floor. She opened the door without knocking, and barely let Sam through before slamming it behind them.

The captain looked up from his desk. "I swear on my career, if the two of you—"

"Chapman is working with the rebellion. He's either about to get himself killed trying to expose corruption within the M.O.D.—" Khlid took a deep breath. "—or he is setting up a trap to kill all of us."

The captain sat there with his mouth hanging open for several seconds. Samuel slowly descended into one of the seats across from Williams and put his face in his hands. Khlid wanted to scream. Only as she said it aloud did the truth of it finally fully hit her.

Khlid went over exactly what had happened, sparing no detail except for the conditions in which

Chapman lived. Concluding, she said, "If it *is* a trap, he's played his hand beautifully. The only place that could confirm or deny Chapman's story is the Ministry of Defense. Since asking them could tip off the murderers, we cannot do that."

Williams opened his clasped hands. "Then you're *advocating* storming a possibly Ministry of Defense-owned factory? Because of a tip from Chapman, who just beat you senseless and has been lying to all of us for God knows how long?"

Khlid knew how she sounded. "Captain, this is happening in our jurisdiction. If it *is* the M.O.D., we have the right to investigate. Especially if it is someone behind a desk abusing their power. We serve the people, and our oaths demand we do whatever is necessary to ensure their safety under the Almighty. No part of that oath says we turn a blind eye when the abuse comes from within."

"And if none of it's true, and Chapman is laying a trap?"

Khlid simply shrugged. "Then he deserves to be arrested."

Williams had sat back in his chair. Samuel had started rubbing her back. A habit he often did when he thought she was in distress.

"If even one iota of what you have said to me here today is untrue, I will personally strip you of your badge, citizenship, and send you off to the questioners at the M.O.D. myself. Am I clear?"

"Yes, Captain."

"Let's say Chapman is right. If we catch M.O.D. murdering civilians, it seems likely to me that the Ministry of Justice would dismantle the Seventh—possibly the Imperial Police Force itself—and bury the story. If we follow Chapman's lead and it takes us where he says it will, the rest of our professional lives will be out of my control. Either the M.O.D. high command will be purged—or we will. Do you understand?"

Samuel and Khlid answered as one, "Yes, Captain."

Williams leaned over his desk. "That only leaves one question. Khlid, do you think Chapman is telling the truth?"

Khlid took several moments to weigh everything that had happened these last few hours. Chapman had lied, but she had a feeling every word he had spoken after confessing his affiliation had been the truth. She had wanted to reject it; it went against her faith in everything she had devoted her life to.

But Chapman had asked for help. Something, to that point, he had shown himself incapable of doing.

"Yes."

Williams stood and opened his office door.

"Rollins! Get in here now." He closed the door and sat back at his desk. "What we're about to do might establish a new precedent for police investigations of the government. We could also be the first precinct to catch rebels. That, or I am about to order my officers into a massacre. Maybe both. Khlid, give me a cigarette."

Khlid blinked at the request but obliged.

The captain took it, dragged on the thing for longer than Khlid thought humanly possible, and said, "We took an oath." Smoke curled around his lips.

Rollins came in and shut the door. "Yes, Captain?"

"Rollins, head to the Ministry of Defense and ask to speak with Captain Viro. Tell him the Seventh Precinct has received information of imminent rebel activity in our jurisdiction at Warehouse Two. We need backup immediately."

Rollins' eyes seemed to nearly bulge out of his head. "Yes, Captain." He turned for the door.

"Rollins, I am not done."

The sergeant snapped back to attention. "Sorry, sir."

"Before that, go to the Ministry of Truth and tell them we need two truth seekers sent to Warehouse Two immediately. That means roughly one hour from now, I expect a full regiment of soldiers at the warehouse gate. Roughly twenty minutes prior to that, two truth seekers should be on the scene. Am I clear?"

"Crystal, sir."

"Fantastic. Now you can go."

Rollins nearly flew out of the room.

"I have never seen him move so fast," Samuel said.

Khlid shot him a look, but he only added, "It's true."

She turned back to the captain. "Sir, what are you planning?"

Williams took one deep breath before answering. "To gamble with your lives. The Seventh are going to raid the warehouse *before* the Ministry has time to send their soldiers. By the time they get there, assuming this is not a trap, we'll have had time to collect evidence of wrongdoing—even if it turns out to be the government's own wrongdoing—without Ministry interference."

"And if it *is* a trap?" Khlid asked.

"Then we only need to hold out long enough for backup to arrive."

Samuel let out a whistle. "We'd better get moving. The Ministries won't waste time once they hear."

Thunder crashed outside.

The captain stood. "Yes. We had better."

THE CAPTAIN'S voice boomed from the second-floor railing over the bustle of officers arming themselves. "Move, move, move! This is a raid. Rifles and ammo. Dowl, where's your jacket? Kallin, get another ammunition belt. Sipmun, if I see you sitting again, I *will* put a boot in your ass." Williams looked down on the preparing officers. He had told them only that rebel activity had been found by Chapman, and that he needed help. Adding the first lie Khlid had ever knowingly heard from Williams to his officers, he told them the rebels might be in possession of Ministry uniforms. If the Ministry did turn out to be in league with the perpetrators, this lie would potentially prevent confusion; but it could backfire just as easily. Tonight would have lasting effects on the future of the Empire—regardless of the outcome.

Khlid and Samuel stood near the back of the desk pool, rifles at the ready. Khlid now wore her freshly cleaned and pressed inspector's coat. A replacement badge had even been brought by an officer moments ago.

She watched the officers with pride. "At this rate, we'll be on our way before the top of the hour."

"Those drills are paying off," Samuel said.

"Mm-hm." Khlid placed a round into her rifle's breech and snapped it shut. "Let's hope Rollins doesn't get to the Ministries too quickly."

A tense silence settled between them.

Sam broke it with, "Are you sure you're up to this? You've been through it today."

"I am barely standing." Khlid laced her fingers through her husband's. "But if you try and get me taken off of this, I'll kill you."

"Ha!" Sam pulled her a little closer. "I will just be sure to watch your back extra close."

Khlid grinned. "Plus, whatever the fucking drug is that Chapman gave me is a work from the Almighty itself. I don't feel a damn thing aside from tired."

"Knowing Chapman, you might not *want* to know exactly what it was."

The silence returned, but Khlid felt no tension.

This time she broke it, saying, "I love you."

Sam squeezed her hand in response. "We really need to get better at staying mad at each other."

"I *am* still mad." She met his eyes. "But we could be about to die, so, priorities."

He smiled down at her. "Priorities."

Khlid and Samuel shared their last kiss.

· · ·

THE THUNDERSTORM WAS one of the worst of the season. Inches of water flowed over the streets. Khlid could not see more than a block in front of her through the downpour. Every minute or so, a crack of lightning lit the entire city.

What a wonderful day for a raid. Khlid was exhausted. She felt certain whatever Chapman had given her was meant to make her tired—possibly to keep her from coming to the raid herself. *Fat chance.* The rifle in her hands was heavier than she ever remembered, but Khlid knew once it all began, adrenaline would be her savior. Already, still a block away from Warehouse Two, a tingling thrill pricked at her.

Thirty officers had been brought to take the warehouse. Ten backed Khlid and Samuel, approaching from the front. Five more would enter through the smaller side doors. The last ten were to watch for runners out the back—a tactic Khlid was a big fan of. Funnel your enemy to an exit which is itself a trap. She had never seen it fail.

Samuel consulted his pocket watch. He signed "two minutes" to all in the alley. Getting so close without being seen had not been easy. They had sprinted the whole way, through pounding rain and side streets and alleys filled with waste, and worse, to avoid detection. Now they crouched, breathing heavily, waiting for the other teams to get in position. At a quarter to the hour, all would make their approach.

Smits approached from the back of the line of officers and said, "Good to go, Inspectors. Though a few of the men need reminding about their required cardio regimen."

"Thank you, Smits," Samuel said.

"Smits," Khlid pulled the man closer. "Tell me honestly, have they been keeping up with their rifle practice?"

"Absolutely, ma'am." Smits let a grin spread across his face. "Easier to get an officer to the firing range than the track; I was at the range last night myself. Just be glad the M.O.D. let us start using cartridges. Dealing with powder in a downpour like this would be impossible."

Khlid nodded and let the officer go. The advancement of weaponry in the last few decades had been extraordinary. Her own breech-loaded rifle was the greatest weapon she had ever fired. It was bulky, yes, but what had once taken minutes now took just a few seconds; all she had to do to reload was flip down a lever and insert a cartridge. As if that weren't enough, these rifles were accurate to almost four hundred meters. Khlid couldn't shoot quite that far with good accuracy herself, but the die-hard snipers of the Seventh certainly could.

Samuel signaled "thirty seconds." Officers shuffled forward in response.

Khlid moved up and peeked around the corner connecting the alley to the street Warehouse Two was on. Four guards stood under an awning keeping watch. They had no visible weapons, but Khlid would bet her career they were concealing small handheld arms.

Samuel got into position behind her as the officers settled into preparatory stillness. Anticipation tensed her entire body. The adrenaline she would need blessedly began to pulse through her veins.

Sam's hand lay on her shoulder. "Ten seconds."

The rain pattered on tin roofs. One of the warehouse guards barked a laugh that echoed through the street.

Sam's hand tapped her shoulder three times. "Go."

Khlid raised her rifle and turned the corner.

The guards were well trained. One spotted her when she was only feet from the alley. He raised a cry of alarm.

Khlid matched his cry with her own call: "Police! On your knees!" As more officers emerged from the alley, the guards went from startled to panicked.

A shot rang out in the night from the other side of the warehouse.

Fuck fuck fuck.

Two of the guards darted for the large door to the right, while the other two went for weapons. Disobeying an officer of God during a raid was punishable by death. Khlid pulled her trigger. Five more shots rang out from behind her.

All four guards dropped. One screamed as he died. Khlid closed the distance while pulling out her sidearm. She ended his pain with a bullet to the head.

Several more shots rang out from the other side of the warehouse yet again.

Are they already fleeing? She snapped open her rifle and replaced the cartridge. "On the door!"

Khlid and the other officers stacked up at the door. Samuel, positioned across from her, began counting down from five, but Khlid stopped him. She gestured behind him to a small ladder leading to a second-floor fire escape. He nodded his agreement. Khlid tapped Smits and they broke off.

Khlid climbed the ladder first, with Smits close behind. Sam watched them climb and waited a hair-raising beat for them to get into place at a window.

The window led to a dark, messy office. Papers were strewn about and the door had been left open. An open box of small-caliber rounds on the desk caught her eye.

"Well, Smits, it looks like resisting arrest will be added to the charges here tonight."

"Yes, ma'am."

Below, Sam gave the count. On five, he battered through the door. Simultaneously, Khlid and Smits separated the window from its cheap lock with a sharp snap.

Below, shots rang out again over Sam's cries of "Police!"

As far as she could tell, she and Smits remained undetected. The commotion below provided more than enough sound cover as they reached the doorway and peered into the hall.

To her right, a closed door at the hall's end. To her left, a man in fine attire leaning against the wall, pistol in hand. He was looking away from Khlid, down a stairwell at the other end of the hall. In a matter of a few seconds, Khlid watched him jump at a shadow, point the weapon down the hall, think better of it, holster the gun, and then raise it again.

Khlid signaled Smits to watch the door to the right, and pushed into the hall. Smits crouched down and trained his rifle there, while Khlid slowly walked up behind the tall man with the pistol.

He was too focused on the noise coming from the bottom of the stairway to notice her approach. She pressed the end of her rifle to the back of his head. The man froze like glass.

"Drop the gun." He did so. "Good. Move and you die. Understand?"

"Yes." His voice cracked with fear.

"How many are in the building?"

"Over a dozen."

The odds are in our favor.

More shots and screams rang out below.

"What is happening here tonight?"

"We were hired to store some carts for the M.O.D. That is all I know."

"If that were all you knew, you wouldn't have armed yourself when you heard someone shout 'Police.' You were prepared to shoot officers of the law to defend a mystery box?"

No response.

A shot rang out from behind. Khlid reacted, kicking the back of her prisoner's knee and driving him to the floor. She rolled up facing the back of the hall and saw a man fall through the doorway Smits had been watching, dead.

Khlid's prisoner reached for his dropped weapon, but before he could do more than grasp it, her rifle was at his temple.

The coward went limp.

She hit him again for his stupidity.

"You okay?" Smits called out. His eyes remained trained on the door.

Good man. "Yes." She pulled a cord from her jacket pocket to bind the man's hands. "Clear that room before we head down." Patting the man down, Khlid found a note. It read, *Eighty-four dead. Two successes. The inspector seems to be taking very well.* A pit formed in her stomach.

"It's Chapman. Something... something's been done to him."

Khlid got to her feet and ran to the back room.

Smits held a woman in a medical coat with her hands up at gunpoint. Tall, dark-haired, the woman seemed disturbingly at ease. Rather than distrustfully eyeing the officer holding her life in his hands, her focus was glued to a shirtless Chapman, restrained in a chair.

An empty syringe hung from his arm. A diseased-looking dark fluid undulated beneath his skin at the injection site, visibly pulsating in his veins. Two similar outbreaks writhed at his neck and armpit. His chest was almost completely overtaken by thick dark roots.

Khlid ran to him. He was conscious, but clearly in far too much pain to comprehend his plight. Soft moans rumbled weakly in his chest. Khlid tugged one of his eyes open. She could see the fluid seeping into them. The tendrils moved as if exploring Chapman's body. She recoiled. Her friend spasmed involuntarily, with such force the wooden chair groaned.

"He's beautiful." The medical woman had an accent Khlid did not recognize. "Most would have begun deforming into monsters by now. He takes it like mother's milk."

"What did you do to him?"

"Ahh." The woman's grin widened. "We had fun playing with the little rebel inspector."

Khlid looked back to Chapman. Aside from the nauseating motion of his flesh around the injection sites, Chapman bore many markings of hurried torture: His fingernails were peeled back. A stab wound was visible at his groin. His right nipple was —Khlid forced herself to stop examining the damage.

Instead she looked to the woman, still grinning with apparent glee at her work.

"Okay. Smits, watch the hall." Khlid approached. The woman didn't flinch as Khlid walked right up to her nose, likely assuming an officer of the law would not assault someone in custody.

She was wrong.

Khlid picked the woman up by the collar and slammed her down on the desk. Into the wall. Into a chair that toppled with her. Back onto the desk. Out into the hall and then back into the office. Within thirty seconds, her grin had disappeared.

"What did you do to him?" Khlid hissed the words, holding the bleeding woman's face within a foot of her own.

"We need as many subjects as we can get." The woman coughed. "After we realized he wouldn't tell us who sent him, we injected him." Another cough, rattling now, with fluid.

Khlid had broken something in the doctor.

Good.

Khlid threw the woman back down onto the desk, crushing a case of the syringes. One, intact, rolled off the desk. Khlid caught it in her free hand, uncapped the needle, and brought it within an inch of the torturer's left eye. "Tell me exactly what this does and why it was put into Lord Pruit, or this goes into that soulless eye."

Petrified, the woman drew a ragged breath. "It makes them beautiful."

"What?"

"Lord Pruit needed to be punished for his disobedience. A message for the rest of his ilk."

"Disobedience? What did he do?"

"He attempted to profit off the Empire. The Empire found a new way to manufacture steel, a breakthrough that could assure the Empire's supremacy for generations. And what did the short-sighted idiot do with it? He tried to tell us how much of it we could take. Signing contracts to sell privately. Now all his plants are ours." She seemed to be gaining confidence as she spoke. "You don't know what's coming tonight. You don't know whose operation this really is. You're all going to die."

"You know." Khlid shoved the woman as hard as she could off the desk onto the floor. She wanted to ask more questions. She wanted more time. But every shot heard below could be the one that killed her husband. "I really don't like tough talk." She pulled her side arm and shot the woman three times.

Khlid walked to Chapman. "I am so sorry." Khlid put her gun to his head. The image of Lord Pruit's twisted form danced before her eyes. Her finger tightened on the trigger.

It's Chapman.

Sliding three replacement shells into her weapon, Khlid walked out into the hall and met Smits' eyes. "Let's move."

The gunfire had died down, but occasionally the crashing open of a door, followed by a series of blasts, would ring out.

Khlid brought her rifle to her shoulder as she moved down the stairwell, Smits only a few steps behind. As she reached the halfway landing, Khlid leaned to see down the hall. A man sprinting in Khlid's direction saw her officer's coat and stumbled into reverse.

"Nope." Khlid raised her rifle and shot the man in the right leg. He had no weapon she could see, so she spared his life.

Down the hall, Khlid heard, "*Stay down!*" Samuel's voice. A shot rang out.

"Let's move."

Smits nodded.

Khlid tied the wrists of the man she had shot. He was no threat, but it was procedure to tie up everyone found on the scene of a raid.

At the end of a long hall, Khlid and Smits came to a thick metal door. Fortunately, whoever Khlid had shot in the leg had latched it from this side. With a simple twist of the lock, the door swung open.

Six officers and Samuel met them on the other side with rifles pointed. As soon as recognition flashed between them, all rifles were brought up.

They were all in the main storage area of the warehouse. Countless barrels and crates lined the walls, separated into stacks by shape and size. Each stack was made uniformly of one type of container. It caused the room to have a disorienting effect: a series of miniature mountains, each composed of identical casks, urns, or baskets; each stacked pristinely, yet asymmetrically, like some kind of cubic alien topography.

A circle of five prisoners, all tied, were watched over by Sam's team.

Samuel approached her. "Are you okay?"

"Yes. You?"

"Unharmed." Samuel let out a shaking breath. "We have one dead and one injured. I left Franklin to watch over them."

Khlid noticed more officers making their way through the man-made mountains. "All accounted for, then?"

"I ordered the other two breaching teams to sweep. I assume no more where you came from?"

She nodded. "Two tied up. Management, I believe. One dead. Any word on what the firing out back was about?"

Samuel shook his head. "We just finished up when you got here. We killed seven. One sweep done and none found hiding, but I'm not satisfied." He turned to his assembled officers. "James, Belinda, Marcus, go make contact with the team out back. Tell them to make a complete perimeter."

The three nodded and jogged towards the back of the warehouse.

"Samuel, what do you make of this?" Khlid could

not shake a feeling they were overlooking something desperately obvious.

Thunder boomed outside. Rain clattered softly, continuously, on Warehouse Two's tin roof.

Sam grabbed Khlid's shoulder and lowered his tone. "This was M.O.D. No question. But they weren't wearing uniforms." He stared at the nearest mountain of wares. "Damned if I know what we're looking for. But we have to open up everything we can and secure anything that looks halfway like evidence before our 'backup' arrives."

Khlid stared hard at the inscrutable labyrinth of containers. To one side, a line of wagons loaded with barrels. "Agreed." Khlid called, "Ekris, crowbar, now."

A woman walked over and passed Khlid the bar. Khlid approached the wagons, inspecting the wood of the barrels loaded upon them. Obviously newer than the rest. Khlid climbed the front wagon and placed the crowbar at the lip of the closest barrel.

This is it. Whatever it is we came here for, it has to be in here.

A gunshot rang out from the back of the warehouse. A single cry. Deafening silence.

Samuel took action. "On me!"

Samuel's six remaining officers formed up behind him, smoothly fanning out into a "V" shape.

Khlid stayed on the wagon and brought her rifle to her shoulder yet again.

A tremendous crash came from the far end of the warehouse, and another series of shots.

"What is happening?" Khlid called. "Marcus, report!"

Only silence. Several beats passed.

Atop a high stack, a barrel wobbled over, then fell. It smashed into others on its descent, creating in short order a cacophonous avalanche, louder than thunder. Several officers lowered their rifles and attempted to cover their ears.

Sam turned to give orders to his team.

Movement caught Khlid's eye. "Sam!"

Her warning came just in time. Sam dropped to his belly and narrowly dodged a mass of something flying through the air. It struck a wagon further down the line from Khlid. The wood of the wagon cracked with the impact, and the mass—the limp body of an officer—fell to the floor.

As the body came to rest, Khlid identified the officer: Franklin. His face looked as if a sledge-hammer had been taken to it.

"Officers of the law interfering with Imperial business?" The voice was liquid, yet sharp. A serpent's hiss. Khlid could assign no age or gender to it. All she knew was it sounded like death.

A figure all in black emerged from behind a stack of crates. She trained her rifle and called out to Sam, "At your two o'clock."

Samuel regained his feet and every officer made a firing line, half of them dropping to one knee.

As the figure approached, Khlid saw a white mask under its capacious hood. The mask's mouth formed a rictus grin with blood-red lips.

"Oh, and threatening one of the Chosen. The police certainly are getting bold. Your man, Rollins, I believe it was. He was much more compliant."

Smits lowered his rifle. "Inspector, what is this?"

Samuel kept his aim true.

"My dear inspector, if you believe I have done wrong, come put that cord on me yourself." The Chosen raised its hands, palms turned to the ceiling. It wore gauntlets with long black claws.

No one moved.

"Is there a problem, Inspector?" The soft voice poisoned the air.

Khlid was frozen. This was one of the Anointed —a Chosen. A human made into a demigod by God. This was not some corrupt M.O.D. operation. The Seventh had overstepped their power and stormed through a warehouse, murdering operatives working in full compliance with Imperial Will. With the Almighty's will.

Samuel had reached the same conclusion. He lowered his rifle, placed it onto the floor, and got down to one knee. "No, Chosen."

"Unfortunately, I think there is."

Khlid knew it was coming. A tear traversed her eyelash. She fired her rifle, but too late. Her round pierced a barrel where the Chosen had stood. Black fluid sprayed out.

The Chosen were as fast as the stories claimed. The black-clawed figure was on Samuel in a blur. Khlid could not track precisely what happened, but in one instant, it lifted Samuel high above its head, and in the next, it rammed those claws through his chest. The bloody black claws protruded from Sam's back, writhing like tentacles, fawning over each other, relishing the gore.

Samuel immediately went limp. He made no sound.

Khlid's husband was dead.

Khlid didn't scream or buckle. She drew her pistol and opened fire. Chest, leg, and stomach. All three shots landed before the thing hurled her husband's body at her. Samuel's limp corpse crashed into Khlid and sent her over the back of the wagon.

Gunshots and screams filled the air as the remaining of the Seventh died.

Khlid hurt all over. Chapman's painkiller was clearly still working—without it, she would hardly have been able to move from the number of bruises and fractures. Instead, she simply clung to the body on top of her. *Sam. Sam, I love you. Please don't leave me.* She kissed his face and pulled him even tighter. "We were stupid, Sam. We shouldn't have come."

Dozens more shots rang out as Khlid clutched Samuel to her chest. She stroked his face, wiping the blood away, and kissed him softly.

Sam, you are my heart.

The last screaming voice was extinguished.

The sound of heavy boots approached. The wagon she had retreated behind was tossed to the side as a child would an unwanted toy. The grinning white mask stared down at her. Khlid noticed gray eyes within.

"Love is a beautiful thing. Is it not, Inspector?"

Khlid closed her eyes and buried her face in Sam's neck. She tensed for what was to come. She hoped it would be quick.

Instead of the sounds of her own flesh being torn to pieces, a guttural growl vibrated in the air. Khlid opened her eyes and looked up. The Chosen's eyes were wide. It turned.

Behind the Chosen among the dead, stood Chapman—what had once been Chapman. Grotesque edges of bone protruded from his body. Fangs several inches long hung from his mouth. His skin had been pulled tight over corded muscle. He had become a walking nightmare.

The beast that was Chapman lunged at Khlid's attacker.

The Chosen nearly fell on top of Khlid as Chapman's jaws seized its throat. She heard claws tearing flesh. The Chosen screamed.

Chapman hurt a Chosen. Disbelief pierced her grief and shock.

The two stumbled away from her as the Chosen tried desperately to fend off the feral creature.

Khlid rolled to her knees and elbows. Her many injuries began to ring more loudly through what remained of the medicine Chapman had given her. She looked into Samuel's still-open eyes. They were blank. The soul of her husband was gone. "Please, Almighty, forgive me." She pushed herself to her feet, and began limping for the exit.

The sounds of the fight changed behind her—a scream of pain with tinges of Chapman's voice.

She was close to the front door. It had been

blasted open, now barely hanging on its hinges. Rain-water poured in from the streets. The downpour outside was like a solid wall.

Khlid reached the exit and spared one look back. She immediately wished she hadn't. A loud, wet, ripping sound filled the air, followed by an unnatural death rattle. The agonized sound an animal makes as it is brutalized by a predator, mixed with demonic growling and unmistakably human wails.

A final *snap*. Now all Khlid could hear was the pounding of the rain outside.

"I am coming, little rabbit. Run as fast as you can."

❧ 6 ❧

THE FLIGHT

Khlid smashed into the saloon door she had spotted through the rain and fell face-first into the brightly lit room. Several women screamed in surprise, and the sounds of pistols drawn immediately replaced the boisterous atmosphere the battered inspector had collapsed into. A piano player slammed his knees into his instrument as he leapt from the keys for his rifle. In the sudden, tense stillness, the only sound was of the rain blowing in behind her through the now broken door.

Years of training told Khlid to roll onto her back and point her gun back toward the rain-battered doorway she had fallen through. Training told her to pick herself up, shout a warning to the patrons, and vanish. Instead, all she managed to do was get on her knees and vomit. Several of those around her made sounds of protest. One man let out an uncomfortable chuckle.

Khlid noticed black worms moving within her spilled bile.

She could not regain herself. Panic overtook any tactical action. Her entire world was the ragged, insufficient breaths she managed to pull in, and the name Samuel, repeating in her mind. Khlid had no idea how long she knelt there on all fours. A panting, wild animal, chased by a predator, unable to flee any further.

Breathe in... breathe out. Breathe in... breathe out. No semblance of calm came. Instead, she began to shiver involuntarily as she processed more of what had happened. *Sam.*

A hand came to rest on Khlid's shoulder. Finally, her training took over. Grabbing the hand, Khlid rolled on top of the assailant and brought her revolver up to their neck. She would have pulled the trigger, too, had the mass of pink frills beneath her not screamed to Khlid's remaining rationality, *not a threat!*

The woman Khlid was now threatening displayed a remarkable lack of perturbation. The human face in front of her finally brought Khlid back into the moment, focused on something real. She identified red lips, dark eyeliner, rosy cheeks, and caution, but not fear. This was a woman used to dealing with sudden spurts of violence. Judging by the hard object Khlid's knee could feel at the woman's hip, she was prepared to do violence of her own if necessary, too.

One of the onlookers said, "Please, let our mother go."

Mother? Khlid finally really looked around. Women in daring dresses, and men in various states of undress, crowded a common room. Drinks had been set down in favor of the small pistols favored by workers in the sex trade. Khlid had barged into a brothel, and judging by the tension in the air, the only reason she had not been shot was her soaking wet officer's uniform.

"Mother," or in some cases "Father," was the term of endearment used by the heads of these legal brothels. The position was actually one of fairly high regard within society. It had to be. Who would dare cross the organizing force behind the workers most highly valued by certain members of the upper class?

Khlid's mind refocused on exactly what had brought her here. She released the mother she had pinned beneath her. The mother, her hands raised in surrender, said, "I would show you our license, but something tells me this is not an inspection."

Khlid's eyes scanned the room, unable to focus. Normally she would evaluate her surroundings, process, and decide what to do next—but every face in the brothel was Samuel's. Some bore the smile she loved; the rest, a blood-smeared oblivion.

The mother got to her feet. "Please, Inspector, lower your weapon."

Khlid realized her pistol was still readied. She had been pointing it at everyone she turned to. She realized, too, that she was weeping silently.

The mother put her hand on Khlid's wrist, pushing her gun hand to her side with the gentlest of suggestions. Khlid didn't resist.

"Dear, what happened to you?"

Khlid looked up from her pistol and met the woman's eyes. "I am not safe." Her gaze must have been unhinged; at these words, the mother took a full step back. "*We* are not safe."

It took only a heartbeat for the mother to sweep into action.

"Grav and Triss," began the mother, solid and commanding, "bar the door. Sitt and Hettus, clear the back alley; make sure the building isn't being watched. If you work here, stay close and armed. The rest of you, we're closing early. Out!"

Khlid could not tell if it took minutes or hours, but soon she was in a back room of the brothel with a crowd of only two: the mother (she had introduced herself as Christi), and her second, a voluptuous, dark-haired man named Brev; both trying to get enough information out of Khlid to know what to do next. Every time Khlid tried to convey what had happened, her mind flinched away and her throat seized. *Samuel!* her mind screamed.

Christi let out a frustrated sigh and turned to Brev. "What in the hell are we caught up in?"

Brev only shrugged in response. It was quite apparent to Khlid that Brev was far from sober, and feeling the effects of something stronger than drink. His twitching and rocking hardly served to ameliorate Khlid's own sense of equilibrium.

Christi closed her eyes and rubbed her temples before looking back to Khlid. "You're an officer of God, all right. You fight like a tactician, not a brawler."

Khlid noted perversely that this mother would make a semi-competent inspector.

"All right," Christi said. "The bars on your shoulder make you an inspector, and the lines on your face tell me you've been one a while." Her frown deepened. "Were you attacked?"

What could she say? Nothing. Nothing came to her mind as a reasonable response. Even if Khlid did somehow explain, why would they not just turn her over? She was a fugitive.

Khlid only nodded.

The mother abruptly turned, grabbed Brev's chin and smacked him hard. She repeated the action twice more before the man finally felt it, moving back and covering his face with his arms. Then Christi grabbed him by the shoulders and made him meet her eyes.

"Tell everyone to get ready to run. Inspectors don't lose their composure like this; that means something bad is coming—bad enough to do this to her. We have to assume whoever they are, that they're still watching, waiting for her to leave or get kicked out of here. The only way we can keep her safe is to all leave at once and head in different directions. Do you understand?"

Brev's eyes seemed to glaze over for a moment, but he snapped back into reality the second Christi's hand went back. "Yes, ma'am."

"Go to the lost and found. Get everyone an unclaimed cloak. Then bring two in here for us."

"Yes, ma'am." And with that, sporting an extraordinary erection, Brev bounded from the room yelling orders.

Christi turned back to Khlid. "We have a fifty-fifty chance he'll remember the cloaks for us. Girl, I don't know what happened to you tonight, but I know every police precinct in the city. The closest is six blocks away."

Khlid focused enough to realize she was a lot more than six blocks from Seventh Precinct headquarters. "*No!*" she said, much too loudly, but with what she had seen tonight. "It has to be the Seventh Precinct. We must make it to the Seventh."

Christi began to protest, but seemed to realize something and closed her mouth. She bent down to look Khlid directly in the eyes. "It's like that, is it?"

Minutes later, the brothel was bustling with people preparing to make an organized dash into the rain. If Khlid had not been in shock, watching a few dozen sex workers scurry out into the night wearing oversized cloaks might have made her laugh. Tonight, the moment the door opened to the torrent outside, she froze in fear. It was out there. The hunter.

It took fairly extreme encouragement from Christi to usher Khlid out the door, but once she did, it took every ounce of her restraint not to start sprinting. They had to walk briskly like everyone else. Nothing to distinguish them from each other.

Water sloshing into her boots, the rain pounding against a borrowed leather cowl, the entire walk was a fear-coated blur to Khlid. She was convinced every breath would be her last. An impossibly fast assassin would swoop down from one of the rooftops and kill her and the mother foolhardy enough to help her before they had time to react. Yet it never happened. They made it all the way to Eighteenth Street without incident. It was not until Christi's pounding on the Seventh Precinct door was answered by a star- tled, fresh-faced officer that Khlid allowed herself to hope she might live through the night. She recog- nized him—his name was Jun—one of three junior recruits left to staff the precinct while the rest of the on-duty officers went on the raid.

Jun protested as the mother tried to push her way inside, which made sense, given that nearly the entire force was out on a raid. It wasn't until Christi pulled Khlid's hood back and revealed her face that Jun relented. His eyes went wide and his face dropped. The implications of her being here, alone, the rain mixing with tears on her bruised face, visibly struck Jun.

He ushered them inside and out of the pouring rain.

7

THE TRUTH

The cigarette Khlid held had nearly burned down to her fingers. She sat on the floor of the interrogation room, her back against the wall. The captain had pulled up one of the two chairs from the table. He sat next to her, wet stains on his cheeks. Khlid had finally managed to recount most of what had happened to the captain, who listened horrified, trying to suppress his shock. When he began to prompt her, attempting to get the information from her faster, she began to sob. As he held her shuddering shoulders, she had at last managed to wail the words, "Sam is dead!" and the captain had gotten very quiet.

Khlid bowed her head, the effort of the admission taking an immediate physical toll. There were no tears left, just a raw, corporeal mourning. The only thing she felt now was a deep and tearing loss. The kind that never truly goes away. She craved Samuel's arms around her now, more than she ever had. His embrace would undo everything that had gone wrong. Facing an invincible enemy would seem manageable with him at her side. Without him, Khlid felt helpless. There wasn't going to be a fight. Just a series of executions.

The particulars of the last few rain- and adrenaline-soaked hours were already fogging over in Khlid's mind. Shock would do that.

Khlid was pretty sure the downpour had saved her life. The Chosen who had chased her was eager to eliminate the last witness. But the storm had evened the odds, obscuring Khlid's path, slick cobbles reducing the Chosen's speed advantage.

Leaning back in his chair, the captain finally broke the silence. "Chapman... was truly a member of the rebellion. He forced us all into a situation where we would see something we weren't supposed to see." Khlid had never seen the man so morose. His eyes looked impossibly sunken.

Khlid let the cigarette fall from her fingers.

"I bought his story... I believed it."

Khlid laid her head back against the wall as fresh tears streamed down her face. Apparently she did have more to spill. *Samuel.*

The captain continued, "Whatever it was that attacked you..." He paused and took a long breath. "No, we can't ignore facts. The way you describe it, that was one of the Anointed."

Khlid broke her silence. "If you say those words outside of this room, you're dead." A pure statement of fact. If officers of the law made accusations of any kind against one of the Anointed, those chosen by the Almighty, they would be killed without trial. It was treason. Even if the accusations were true, an Anointed could do as they pleased. They were not bound by law or Ministry. Only the orders of the Almighty. Samuel's summary murder had been absolutely within the bounds of Imperial Right. The only one who might be punished would be Khlid, for having left the scene.

The captain nodded. "And that's why we have to get you out of the city. For good. Your life here is done. After today, you will no longer even know the name Khlid. Do you understand?"

Khlid took her time processing what she had just heard: a precinct captain, offering to help a fugitive of the Empire escape the city. If he was caught, he would be tried and killed. His family name would be branded for generations.

Khlid said softly, "You can't."

"I very damn well can. More than half my men

were taken today, and I doubt I will ever fully know why." Anger bled into his voice as he stood and began pacing the room. "I am a loyal servant of the Empire, but I will not let them get you, too." His eyes drifted off. Khlid wasn't entirely sure he was not in mild shock. "They can't take you, too."

Khlid stood and walked over to Williams. He turned to her in slight surprise, escalating to an actual gasp of discomfort as she hugged him. Khlid had looked up to the captain her entire career. He also happened to be a damned good person. And this would have to be goodbye.

Awkwardly, the captain returned her embrace. "You and Sam were the best this precinct ever had."

He let her go and cleared his throat with discomfort. "We have to get you out of the city. My career is over for sending my men in there tonight, but I can pass off some of the responsibility. My trusted inspector, Chapman, convinced me there were rebels in there; the rest, a dreadful misunderstanding. Hell, it's halfway true, anyway. Just shy of grounds for execution."

Khlid nodded in response and folded her arms. As comforting thoughts went, it was going to have to do.

Williams walked to the table and picked up Khlid's service revolver. Agitated as she had been when she first arrived, he'd taken it as a precaution. Now, he checked to make sure it was loaded, added six shots from his own belt, and handed it over. "I have a feeling you may need this."

Khlid took the gun and holstered it. The added weight felt right. After all these years of wearing the thing ten hours a day, more, she felt naked without it. Having it back reinforced her growing resolve to survive and...

Holy shit. I am going to join the rebels.

She had not consciously thought it, but it had been her plan since she stepped into the rain from the warehouse.

Captain Williams walked past her to the door and opened it. "You will need to grab a change of clothes from the back; civilian garb. We will take you through the..." He trailed off and froze. He stopped so abruptly, Khlid nearly walked into his broad back as she followed him out to the desk pool.

A chill grabbed Khlid's spine. She knew what she would see when she looked past the captain. Her resolve crumbled as she saw the figure in black, standing in the middle of the room, staring directly at her. The same white mask with the rictus grin mesmerized her. She could not pull her eyes from it.

The three of them stood there for what felt like an eternity, but could not have been more than a few seconds. It was the hunter, the Anointed, who broke the silence first. Its voice was no louder than a whisper, but it somehow boomed off of every wall. The sound consumed her mind with its soft, deadly tone.

"If you had simply stayed and died, they would have lived." It nodded its head slightly to the left as it spoke.

Khlid looked where the Anointed had motioned. At the far end of the room, Christi and Jun, as well as the two other officers still in the precinct, were all seated neatly at individual desks in a line. Jun's head was twisted until it faced the wrong way. Christi's mouth was raised to the ceiling, an officer's decorative saber pushed from the back of her skull and through her parted red lips. One officer had a pistol pushed into his eye socket. The last was missing his throat, blood still flowing down his chest.

After giving Khlid and Williams a moment to appreciate everything it had done, the Anointed spoke again: **"This is your fault, little rabbit."**

"Why?" the captain asked. His voice did not sound angry, or even upset. It only contained defeat.

"We really didn't think you were competent enough to find us." It was said with both mirth and vitriol. **"It was that Chap-**

man, I assume. He's a clever one. Pulling from two pools of knowledge? I should have congratulated him but—" The Anointed looked back to the dead sitting at their desks. Before it could say more, the captain capitalized on the move.

Khlid had heard the captain was a fast and accurate shot in his heyday, but what she saw was beyond her highest expectations. In the beat of a heart, Captain Williams drew and fired his pistol at the Anointed. The mask cracked with a spray of blood. The captain took aim again, but before he could fire a second shot, the Anointed spun. A knife flew from beneath a spiraling black cloak. The blade shot clean through the captain's chest. A thud came from the wall behind Khlid.

The captain dropped without a cry.

It all happened so fast, Khlid had only managed to get a hand on her pistol. She drew and fired, but the Anointed was prepared now. It easily moved out of the way of her shot.

The Anointed spun again.

A knife shattered Khlid's right knee. Screaming, she collapsed to the floor.

The sound of boots approaching.

The black-cloaked Chosen kicked her like a child's ball. Khlid flew through the air and crashed into the far wall. The snapping of her spine was the last thing she felt. Numbness flooded her body.

Heavy black boots made a slow approach at the edges of her vision. The Chosen dropped its ruined mask to the floor. Blood dripped over the grin as the face stared at her.

The Chosen rolled Khlid over with one foot.

Turning her eyes upwards, Khlid saw the face of her husband's killer for the first and last time. Gray eyes set in a beautiful woman's face stared down at her. **"We do need more subjects, little rabbit. It seems you have earned the honor."**

Khlid's last thought was that she had spent the last few weeks sleeping alone in her apartment, waiting for Sam to get back from that stupid chicken case. She would never get to wake up next to him again.

A boot filled her vision and then, nothing.

8

THE COVERUP

Jotch Holdir sat at his desk at the Ministry of Truth and stared at the report that had just been handed to him. It was his job to take the *Letters of Truth,* as they were called, and write them into articles to be published throughout the Empire. This was the first time he had been handed a first-class story. It was a massive opportunity, one he had been eagerly waiting for for three years now.

The problem was, Jotch knew this letter was a lie.

Last night, his half brother Michael, a rather popular prostitute, had come by late at night and told him a magnificent story of an Imperial inspector on the run. The woman had apparently been chased by someone that scared the ever-loving hell out of her. He had been clear that the woman was in a state of complete terror and had been escorted by Mother Christi, his boss, back to her precinct.

Michael excitedly brought this story to his brother, thinking he could write about it for the paper. Jotch had told Michael he would need to gather more evidence first. He promised if he could track down this mysterious inspector in distress and get a full account, he would run it in his personal column. His half brother had left with a smile on his face, excited to have possibly given Jotch his first big story.

Now, the letter in front of Jotch claimed his brother had died last night in a fire at the brothel, well before he had shown up at his door. The fire had supposedly been set by members of the rebellion. In a simultaneous hit, the rebels had apparently burned the entire Seventh Precinct. It went on to claim three traitorous inspectors named Khlid Whitter, Samuel Whitter, and Chapman Hilt lured most of their precinct into a trap at a long-abandoned warehouse. None had survived.

"The Ministry of Defense is cooperating with the Ministry of Truth to get to the bottom of this latest attack by the rebellion. Why they chose these targets is

unknown. The Ministries have faith in the vision of the Almighty. Justice will be brought."

At the bottom of the *Letter of Truth* was a note instructing Jotch to invite any witnesses to come forward to the Ministry of Truth directly, in order to help the Empire seek justice for what had been done. Jotch had written such invitations dozens of times before. With what he saw now, every single one of them twisted in his memory.

A tear landed on the letter lying on his desk. Jotch realized he was hunched over it, crying. *Michael is dead.* The full realization hit him like a hammer. His brother had been murdered to cover something up. What, Jotch might never know.

A million ideas spun through his head. He would write the discrepancies and publish—

He would publish nothing. His editor was an absolute loyalist and would have Jotch hauled off for even hinting at what he knew. *I'll go down to the brothel and—*

If he acted out of line in any way, it would bring scrutiny. Somehow, the fact that Michael was his half brother had been missed. If they found out now, Jotch would be disappeared, too.

Another tear hit the letter. Michael would never come to his door again to gossip about the weird proclivities of the noble class that frequented his services. They would never again go on holiday with their family in the country. Michael was gone forever.

A third tear hit the letter. Jotch laid his hands on his typewriter, and began writing lies.

ACKNOWLEDGMENTS

Thank you to everyone who supported me in this fantastic writing journey. I would not be here today if not for the support of my friends, family, and subscribers.

ABOUT THE AUTHOR

Daniel Greene is a fantasy YouTuber, entertainer, and with the publication of this book, author. He is known for his video reviews of various science fiction/fantasy works, and love of The Wheel of Time. You may also know him by his moniker, The Disheveled Goblin. You can find him posting videos to YouTube Monday thru Friday. All you have to do is search his name.

 twitter.com/DanielBGreene

 instagram.com/dgreene101

 youtube.com/DanielGreeneReviews